Pageant

Forms of Drama

Forms of Drama meets the need for accessible, mid-length volumes that offer undergraduate readers authoritative guides to the distinct forms of global drama. From classical Greek tragedy to Chinese pear garden theatre, cabaret to *kathakali,* the series equips readers with models and methodologies for analysing a wide range of performance practices and engaging with these as 'craft'.

SERIES EDITOR: SIMON SHEPHERD

Cabaret
978-1-3501-4025-7
William Grange

Pageant
978-1-3501-4451-4
Joan FitzPatrick Dean

Satire
978-1-3501-4007-3
Joel Schechter

Tragicomedy
978-1-3501-4430-9
Brean Hammond

Pageant

Joan FitzPatrick Dean

methuen | drama

LONDON • NEW YORK • OXFORD • NEW DELHI • SYDNEY

METHUEN DRAMA
Bloomsbury Publishing Plc
50 Bedford Square, London, WC1B 3DP, UK
1385 Broadway, New York, NY 10018, USA
29 Earlsfort Terrace, Dublin 2, Ireland

BLOOMSBURY, METHUEN DRAMA and the Methuen Drama logo are
trademarks of Bloomsbury Publishing Plc

First published in Great Britain 2021

Series design by Charlotte Daniels

A catalogue record for this book is available from the British Library.

Library of Congress Control Number: 2021938156

ISBN: HB: 978-1-3501-4452-1
         PB: 978-1-3501-4451-4
         ePDF: 978-1-3501-4454-5
         eBook: 978-1-3501-4453-8

Series: Forms of Drama

Typeset by Integra Software Services Pvt. Ltd.
Printed and bound in Great Britain

To find out more about our authors and books visit www.bloomsbury.com
and sign up for our newsletters.

For Colin Matthew Davis

CONTENTS

LIST OF
ILLUSTRATIONS

SERIES PREFACE

The scope of this series is scripted aesthetic activity that works by means of personation.

Scripting is done in a wide variety of ways. It may, most obviously, be the more or less detailed written text familiar in the stage play of the Western tradition, which not only provides lines to be spoken but directions for speaking them. Or it may be a set of instructions, a structure or scenario, on the basis of which performers improvise, drawing, as they do so, on an already learnt repertoire of routines and responses. Or there may be nothing written, just sets of rules, arrangements, and even speeches orally handed down over time. The effectiveness of such unwritten scripting can be seen in the behaviour of audiences, who, without reading a script, have learnt how to conduct themselves appropriately at the different activities they attend. For one of the key things that unwritten script specifies and assumes is the relationship between the various groups of participants, including the separation, or not, between doers and watchers.

What is scripted is specifically an aesthetic activity. That specification distinguishes drama from non-aesthetic activity using personation. Following the work of Erving Goffman in the mid-1950s, especially his book *The Presentation of Self in Everyday Life*, the social sciences have made us richly aware of the various ways in which human interactions are performed. Going shopping, for example, is a performance in that we present a version of ourselves in each encounter we make. We may indeed have changed our clothes before setting out. This, though, is a social performance.

The distinction between social performance and aesthetic activity is not clear-cut. The two sorts of practice overlap and mingle with one another. An activity may be more or less aesthetic, but the crucial distinguishing feature is the status of the aesthetic element. Going shopping may contain an aesthetic element – decisions about clothes and shoes to wear – but its purpose is not deliberately to make an aesthetic activity or to mark itself as different from everyday social life. The aesthetic element is not regarded as a general requirement. By contrast a court-room trial may be seen as a social performance, in that it has an important social function, but it is at the same time extensively scripted, with prepared speeches, costumes, and choreography. This scripted aesthetic element assists the social function in that it conveys a sense of more than everyday importance and authority to proceedings which can have life-changing impact. Unlike the activity of going shopping, the aesthetic element here is not optional. Derived from tradition it is a required component that gives the specific identity to the activity.

It is defined as an activity in that, in a way different from a painting of Rembrandt's mother or a statue of Ramesses II, something is made to happen over time. And, unlike a symphony concert or firework display, that activity works by means of personation. Such personation may be done by imitating and interpreting – 'inhabiting' – other human beings, fictional or historical, and it may use the bodies of human performers or puppets. But it may also be done by a performer who produces a version of their own self, such as a stand-up comedian or court official on duty, or by a performer who, through doing the event, acquires a self with special status as with the *hijras* securing their sacredness by doing the ritual practice of *badhai*.

Some people prefer to call many of these sorts of scripted aesthetic events not drama but cultural performance. But there are problems with this. First, such labelling tends to keep in place an old-fashioned idea of Western scholarship that drama, with its origins in ancient Greece, is a specifically European 'high' art. Everything outside it is then potentially, and damagingly, consigned to a domain which may be neither 'art' nor 'high'. Instead the European stage play and its like can best be regarded as a subset of the general category, distinct from the rest in that two groups of people come together in order specifically to present and watch a story being acted out by imitating other persons and settings. Thus, the performance of a stage play in this tradition consists of two levels of activity using personation: the interaction of audience and performers and the interaction between characters in a fictional story.

The second problem with the category of cultural performance is that it downplays the significance and persistence of script, in all its varieties. With its roots in the traditional behaviours and beliefs of a society script gives specific instructions for the form – the materials, the structure, and sequence – of the aesthetic activity, the drama. So too, as we have noted, script defines the relationships between those who are present in different capacities at the event.

It is only by attending to what is scripted, to the form of the drama, that we can best analyse its functions and pleasures. At its most simple analysis of form enables us to distinguish between different sorts of aesthetic activity. The masks used in *kathakali* look different from those used in *commedia dell'arte*. They are made of different materials, designs, and colours. The roots of those differences lie in their separate cultural traditions and systems of living. For similar reasons the puppets of *karagoz* and *wayang* differ. But perhaps more importantly the attention to form provides a basis for exploring the operation and effects of a particular work. Those who regularly participate in and watch drama, of whatever sort, learn to recognize and remember the forms of what they see and hear. When one drama has family resemblances to another, in its organization and use of materials, structure, and sequences, those who attend it develop expectations as to how it will – or indeed should – operate. It then becomes possible to specify how a particular work subverts, challenges, or enhances these expectations.

Expectation doesn't only govern response to individual works, however. It can shape, indeed has shaped, assumptions about which dramas are worth studying. It is well established that Asia has ancient and rich dramatic traditions, from the Indian sub-continent to Japan, as does Europe, and these are studied with enthusiasm. But there is much less widespread activity, at least in Western universities, in relation to the traditions of, say, Africa, Latin America, and the Middle East. Second, even within the recognized traditions, there are assumptions that some dramas are more 'artistic', or indeed more 'serious', 'higher' even, than others. Thus, it may be assumed that *noh* or classical tragedy will require the sort of close attention to craft which is not necessary for mumming or *badhai*.

Both sets of assumptions here keep in place a system which allocates value. This series aims to counteract a discriminatory value system by ranging as widely as possible across world practices and by giving the same sort of attention to all the forms it features. Thus book-length studies of forms such as *al-halqa*, *hana keaka*, and *ta'zieh* will appear in English for perhaps the first time. Those studies, just like those of *kathakali*, tragicomedy, and the rest, will adopt the same basic approach. That approach consists of an historical overview of the development of a form combined with, indeed anchored in, detailed analysis of examples and case studies. One of the benefits of properly detailed analysis is that it can reveal the construction which gives a work the appearance of being serious, artistic, and indeed 'high'.

What does that work of construction is script. This series is grounded in the idea that all forms of drama have script of some kind and that an understanding of drama, of any sort, has to include analysis of that script. In taking this approach, books in this series again challenge an assumption which has in recent times governed the study of drama. Deriving from the supposed, but artificial, distinction between cultural performance and drama, many accounts of cultural performance ignore its scriptedness and assume that the proper way of studying it is simply to describe how its practitioners behave and what they make. This is useful enough, but to leave it at that is to produce something that looks like a form of lesser anthropology. The description of behaviors is only the first step in that it establishes what the script is. The next step is to analyse how the script and form work and how they create effect.

But it goes further than this. The close-up analyses of materials, structures, and sequences – of scripted forms – show how they emerge from and connect deeply back into the modes of life and belief to which they are necessary. They tell us in short why, in any culture, the drama needs to be done. Thus by adopting the extended model of drama, and by approaching all dramas in the same way, the books in this series aim to tell us why, in all societies, the activities of scripted aesthetic personation – dramas – keep happening, and need to keep happening.

I am grateful, as always, to Mick Wallis for helping me to think through these issues. Any clumsiness or stupidity is entirely my own.

Simon Shepherd

ACKNOWLEDGMENTS

The epigraph is from *The Tudor and Stuart Monarchy* © Roy Strong. Reproduced by kind permission of Felicity Bryan Literary Agency and the author. The illustration of *A Pageant of Great Women* from the *Yorkshire Telegraph and Star* © The British Library Board, British Newspaper Archive. Quotations from the Ellen Terry/Edith Craig Archive are by kind permission of the National Trust.

My research has been supported by the Department of English at the University of Missouri-Kansas City. Audrey Lester provided invaluable experience and assistance. Thanks to Virginia Blanton, Laurie Ellinghausen, and Jennifer Phegley for encouraging my work and for chairing the department, an especially thankless job, between 2018 and 2021.

I am grateful to the librarians and archivists at the Newberry Library in Chicago, the Theatre and Performance Archives of the Victoria and Albert Museum, the Women's Library at the London School of Economics, the [UK] National Trust, and Special Collections at Northwestern University. Special thanks to Alexander Lock at the British Library, Beverley Cook at the Museum of London, Paul Dudman at the University of East London, Frances Horner at the National Theatre Archive, Melanie Geustyn at the National Library of South Africa, and Shawna White, Curator at the Town of Aurora, Ontario, Canada, for their very generous assistance. I owe a special debt to all the librarians and staff at the University of Missouri-Kansas City, especially Mary Anderson, Larry Ruzich, John Hern, and Liz Johnson.

I also want to thank Pat McKeown, José Lanters, Keith Hopper, Steve Gent, and Seán Moran. Marianne Wells along with my UMKC colleagues Virginia Blanton and Jane Greer read sections of the manuscript and for their suggestions I am very grateful, although any errors are mine alone.

I greatly enjoyed and benefited from the wise counsel, warm collegiality, and steady encouragement of Simon Shepherd, the series editor of Forms of Drama. I am sincerely grateful to Linsey Hague for her diligence, range of knowledge, and care in copyediting.

My enduring gratitude for an eternity of Wednesdays. Rave on.

My greatest thanks go to my family: my brother Christopher, who provided much-appreciated technical support, and my sister Margaret. My daughter Flannery helped in many ways, especially in accessing materials during the pandemic. (I'm still not apologizing for that costume I made for your Noah pageant.) Flannery, her sister Margaret, Phoebe, Darcy, Colin, and Jack continue to change my life and only for the better.

ABBREVIATIONS

AFL	Actresses' Franchise League
APA	American Pageant Association
ASL	Artists' Suffrage League
BL	British Library
ET/EC	Ellen Terry/Edith Craig Archive
IOC	International Olympic Committee
IPC	International Paralympic Committee
LOCOG	London Organising Committee for the Olympic Games
MA/NUIG	Macnas Archive, National University of Ireland-Galway
NUWSS	National Union of Women's Suffrage Societies
WFL	Women's Freedom League
WL/LSE	Women's Library at the London School of Economics
WSPU	Women's Social and Political Union
WWSL	Women's Writers Suffrage League

Inevitably such a subject as pageantry is an interdisciplinary one embracing literature, art, history and iconography. ... whenever I read papers to Professor S. T. Bindoff's seminar at the Institute of Historical Research they were received with what I can only describe as amused tolerance. He once remarked, "When we receive your thesis I suppose as we open it a triumphal arch will pop up."

(Strong 1995: xix–xx)

Introduction

Pageants are a theatrical idiom, often the most public of dramatic forms. They typically seek the widest possible audience—hundreds, thousands, and in the case of the opening ceremony of the 2012 Olympic Games, perhaps 900 million. Pageants also have been performed at royal courts to small, elite audiences, but in all iterations, pageants carry political meaning. As many have observed, pageants perform power. A useful distinction, however, exists between hegemonic and counter-hegemonic pageants. By portraying established power structures as legitimate, perhaps even God-given, hegemonic pageants affirm the status quo. Counter-hegemonic pageants, on the other hand, challenge prevailing authorities to agitate and to advocate for change—the enfranchisement of women, the end of colonial rule, or the freedom of worship. Audiences for counter-hegemonic pageants are more self-selecting than most and, as such, their horizon of expectations is better developed, sharper. Whereas hegemonic pageants incline toward the solemn and the conservative, counter-hegemonic pageants often tap into the subversive impulses of the carnivalesque. Counter-hegemonic pageants appear almost exclusively in liberal societies that tolerate open dissent and free speech; they exist primarily in the modern period.

Theater history is generally told in terms of text-based, published plays. Pageants were only occasionally printed and then only as *objets*, souvenirs, part of a fundraising material culture, not consumed as dramatic texts would be. Even modern pageants may have left not a text, but only fugitive traces: programs, sketches, diary entries, photographs, costume designs, reportage. A "script" or scenario outline might be included in a published program, but pageants are less dependent on text than conventional plays. Created to suit the moment, most pageants were intended for neither publication nor revival. Often their short shelf life only made them especially revelatory of the cultural moment they addressed.

In common parlance, the words "theatre" and "stage" refer to enclosed architectural spaces, but pageants are often performed outside purpose-built theaters. Instead, they appropriate spaces, usually public and often site-specific ones. Contemporary historians, Pierre Nora among them, describe these manipulations of the past as *lieu de mémoire*: "If the expression *lieu de mémoire* must have an official definition, it should be this: a *lieu de mémoire* is any significant entity, whether material or non-material in nature, which by dint of human will or the work of time has become a symbolic element of the memorial heritage of any community" (Nora and Kritzman 1996: xvii). Many pageants were performed outdoors, where, as Ralph Davol wrote, "the pageant stage is limited only by the horizon" (1914b: 301).

Whereas playwrights may challenge or be constrained by theater conventions, a prevailing convention governing pageants is the pursuit of novelty. Pageant producers create ever more surprising, unexpected dramaturgical features, often by exploiting new technologies to amaze and to enthrall their audiences. At some moment in the long life of the York mystery cycle, someone realized that the pageant could create a sensation using a harness and pulleys so that God might fly between his *locus* in heaven above and the main platform playing area. Much to the delight of sell-out audiences, the Irish Free State Army reenacted the Easter Rising by setting ablaze a half-scale replica of Dublin's General Post Office every evening for five consecutive nights in 1935. In *Isles of Wonder*, the Queen appears to parachute to the stadium from a helicopter. Perhaps because such innovations are often dismissed as gimmicks, pageants rarely received the same coverage as conventional drama in media or in scholarship. Seldom reviewed by theater critics, pageants when reported are often covered as social events, subversive demonstrations, or populist gatherings rather than as theater.

Pageants seek out overt theatricality and innovative spectacle to instruct and to delight their audiences. With the notable exception of the medieval cycle plays, pageants may exist entirely outside constraining dramatic conventions. They have no intent of "holding as 'twere a mirror up to nature." Pageants deploy extravagant effects to elicit the visceral responses—the fervent desire for Christian salvation or female enfranchisement, for instance—to which their audiences are already predisposed.

Although a surprising number survive in the archive, Diane Taylor's observation that "live performance can never be captured or transmitted through the archive" (2003: 20) is especially relevant to pageants. Masks, "authentic" costumes, fire, weapons and implements, sensational displays of colorful flags and banners can create spectacles that thrill audiences. This is as true today as it was when Inigo Jones or Leonardo created elaborate masques, the "court hieroglyphics," for Renaissance courts. Exotic costumes, military uniforms, and other distinctive clothing, often made of locally sourced fabrics, identify those who play central roles. Performed in the open air and at night, pageants may employ the spectacular effects of *son et lumière* through the use of powerful searchlights, enveloping LED displays, bonfires, torches, fireworks, and other pyrotechnics. Any appreciation of a pageant depends on one of its most intangible and ephemeral qualities: its aural dimension. Pageants avail of the widest array of auditory sensation possible: song, silence, chanting, gunfire, instrumental music, sound effects, shouting, drumming, chanting, and explosions play key affective roles. This auditory dimension is perhaps the most elusive, the most difficult to document. An orchestra was mandated for *A Pageant of Great Women* but when and what it played remains uncertain. Before the technologies that enable the amplification of sound, pageants often relied on the repetition of episodes before a segment of the audience that could hear the spoken dialogue. In the medieval cycle plays, episodes staged on a wagon might be performed several times as the pageant wagon moved from audience to audience, most famously in the instance of the York cycle. Closer to the present day, newsreel footage and even full audio and visual recordings suggest how inadequately a pageant is judged without hearing all of its aural components. Gunpowder, incense, cordite, or bonfires might even evoke the olfactory sense. Gestures of communal exchange such as handshakes, the linking of arms, or other physical contact stimulate the sensation of touch. By creating sensory overload, pageants reclaim the theatricality of drama. As the text recedes, spectacle comes to dominate.

Through deliberately intense, systematic stimulation, pageantry privileges the sensory over the cerebral, the affective over the intellectual. By creating a spectacular *mise en scène*, pageants cast the action they represent as a defining moment: the salvation of humankind, the ennobling of ancestors, the ascendancy of the monarch. Because pageant episodes may cover hundreds or even thousands of years, the sole character to provide continuity may be a fully reliable, omniscient narrator. In medieval drama, the Crier or Expositor served a similar function, as did Woman in *A Pageant of Great Women*. Especially after the advent of sound amplification, often only a narrator or an announcer has dialogue. Pageant plots are of necessity straightforward and more presentational than representational.

The epic scale to which pageantry aspires employs an entirely different economy than does commercial theater. When public spaces are appropriated, admission might not be charged or charged only for prized seats. Massive pageant casts are fundamentally unlike those in mainstream plays. A key factor to distinguish pageants from other theatrical idioms is amateur performativity. Especially significant were the many times ordinary people, including children and adolescents, were drawn into the act of personation, even if only by carrying a spear. David Rockwell's 2006 book, *Spectacle*, visually documents that the appetite for immense communal gatherings, many of which feature pageants, is undiminished in the digital age. If anything, the advent of social media may have heightened the allure of bodily participation in events such as the opening ceremony of the Olympic Games, Burning Man, or a march on Washington, DC.

Pageants aim to inspire and sometimes, especially when counter-hegemonic, to persuade. Medieval cycle pageants imparted and developed a general knowledge of key biblical episodes to an overwhelmingly preliterate audience. At a time when the liturgy of the Mass was spoken in a language that most people did not understand, pageants staged an accessible narrative of Christianity performed by the laity in the vernacular. In reenacting episodes from the near or distant past, pageants aspire to create or recast a heritage and an identity that audiences can embrace. All pageants aim to entertain while instructing; most incorporate symbolic elements and build on the familiar. By appropriating and transforming familiar sites, pageants endowed sites with a hieratic or even sacred dimension. For medieval pageants, city streets in York, for instance, provided the staging areas for the pageant wagons. From 1377, the London conduits, the sources of public water supply, "formed the emblematic centre of London at times of pageant or royal entry. They created a blessed space" (Ackroyd 2011: 102). Central features of daily life, the conduits were transformed from ordinary to extraordinary for episodes in pageants celebrating coronations or royal entries (Kipling 1997: 64–5). Elaborately decorated arches, intersecting above a prime location, might designate a playing area. The Thames river was the setting for extravagant water pageants in the sixteenth and seventeenth centuries.

Most pageant performers play their parts through their bodily presence, typically rehearsed, coordinated, and highly choreographed on a monumental scale. The synchronized mass movement of large cohorts, a hallmark of many pageants, demonstrates the disciplined commitment of the many performers. Appearing in spectacles like the American Constitution Ratification pageants in the late 1780s or Cicely Hamilton's suffrage pageant in 1910 could be a memorable experience for any participant, especially for the humbler ones. Although the communal spirit of the pageant attracts enthusiasts and amateur talents, unpaid supernumeraries may participate by dint of obligation or coercion. The medieval guilds in towns like York were required by law to perform their part in the mystery cycle and a tax was levied on members of the guild whatever their enthusiasm for the undertaking. Some military tattoos featured pageants; here, too, the element of volition for enlisted men and women is questionable. For many Catholic school students, participation in the annual nativity pageant was not optional. For millions of citizens in the Soviet Union, performance in the October Revolution commemorations was anything but voluntary.

Most pageants restrict the number of speaking roles. The large number of amateur pageant participants is very often supplemented by a small cadre of experienced or professional actors, musicians, dancers, and other theater practitioners. Usually these professionals are entrusted with substantial dialogue or demanding musical performances. Pageants very rarely develop characters of depth and nuance, an ambition common to many theatrical forms. The Hamlets, Willy Lomans, and Antigones of theater history do not emanate from pageants. Instead, pageant characters are usually drawn from history, specifically from a history familiar to the audience. These may be biblical patriarchs, mythological gods, historical personages, abstract figures, or folkloric characters, but the audience has likely heard their name and probably has some sense of their place in history. Boadicea was nearly a fixture of British historical pageants at the beginning of the twentieth century, as was Uncle Sam in American pageants of that period. In many instances, there was no continuity of character across episodes, only a multiplicity of characters who did not interact. In the case of the medieval cycles, God and the Devil appear in different pageants performed by different actors. Pageant-makers often draw on what in Jean Genet's *The Balcony* is called the "Nomenclature," a repository of figures in a particular culture that are clearly recognized but not individualized. Pageantry minimizes what Constantin Stanislavski and most theater practitioners call acting. Much more typically, especially in modern historical pageants, the majority of participants have no individuality, but belong to a large group of hundreds or thousands of performers doing the same thing—marching, dancing, performing calisthenics—often with an astounding, highly rehearsal simultaneity as in the opening ceremony to the 2008 Beijing Olympics.

Pageants typically rely heavily on pastiche, incorporating familiar music, poems, speeches, songs, vernacular forms, and iconic images. They seize upon common knowledge, a fragmentary understanding of the past already widely shared in the audience, and shape those fragments into overarching narratives. With often complete disregard of historical "fact," pageants configure carefully selected historical moments to gratify the audience's preconceptions. Many pageants are populist spectacles designed to give people what they want and often charge them admission to see it. Pageants engender a very different horizon of expectations that, especially after 1600, may incline to the carnivalesque rather than the reverential. Audiences become the inheritors of the past staged in the pageant. Often, there is more singing than dialogue as performers incorporate well-known songs or hymns, possibly inviting the audience to express solidarity by joining in. Pageants offer not only their cast members, but also their large audiences performative opportunities to enact their affiliations and aspirations.

Pageants often celebrate the place where they are performed, the people who perform them, and even the audiences who witness the performance. Some pageants portray the present as the culmination of a continuous past. In Ireland in the first half of the century, for example, the March of the Nation, a parade of proto-Irish republicans from Cuchulain and Brian

Boru through Robert Emmett and Thomas Davis to Michael
Collins, was a regular trope in historical pageants, especially
those performed by the advanced nationalists before 1922 and
by the Defence Forces after Irish Independence. In *Heirs to
the Charter* (1939), a series of vignettes representing pivotal
developments in labor history culminates with the introduction
of Harry Pollitt, "an actual presence as apotheosis" (Wallis
1995: 30). Especially when state-sponsored or subsidized,
pageants can readily become propaganda.

Pageant audiences are likewise unlike other theatre
audiences. The audience sought by historical pageants is rarely
the intelligentsia or the cognoscenti, but rather the ordinary
citizens, especially impressionable, young ones. Against a
natural landscape, in sporting arenas and sometimes in school
halls, pageants may attract spectators who are less than *au fait*
with mainstream theatre; some may never have seen a play.
Some might attend a pageant only in support of one of the
many performers; others, merely to support the charity that
will benefit from the profits. Many pageants were written for
audiences unfamiliar with "the theatre" as an artistic medium.
A defining feature of the large audience for pageants, unlike
most theatrical genres, but like pantomimes and circuses, is the
welcome typically extended to children and adolescents. Since
the twentieth century, pageant-making has been used by schools,
youth organizations, and religious groups as an activity edifying
to their participants and viewers alike. The association with
children and adolescents is yet another reason that pageants
have been relegated to the footnotes of theatre history.

The dynamic between spectator and spectacle in a pageant
may be quite unlike that of a mainstream drama performed
in a purpose-built theatre. A conventional playhouse usually
demands a wholly different decorum from an audience
ensconced in assigned (and often expensive) seats than does
a stadium or an open-air venue. Pageant spectators may also
display their affinity with the production through clothing,
ornament, jewelry, or other identifying markers such as the
white, green, and purple of the WSPU. Lapel accessories,

including pins for those who attended the opening ceremony of the 2012 Olympics, flags, flowers, and the like, all express an allegiance that might blur the barrier between actor and audience. When performed in conventional halls, theatres, or stadiums, pageants may move off a designated playing area, deliberately effacing the barrier between spectator and spectacle to bring the figures personated in more immediate contact with the audience. In at least some productions of *A Pageant of Great Women*, the women of history would process through the auditorium and return to the stage. At the opening ceremony of the 2012 London Olympic Games, huge blue cloths swept over the stadium audience to initiate them into *Isles of Wonder*. In celebrating their enactors as well as those enacted and even those witnessing the enactment, historical pageantry blurs the distinction between actor and audience. Pageants tap emotional chords in the audience, in hope of inspiring the audience to embrace a version of its identity.

The meaning of the word "pageant" has evolved over centuries. In medieval England, "pageant" could refer to the portable stage, often constructed on a wagon, where individual episodes, such as Abraham's sacrifice of Isaac, the birth of Christ, or the Resurrection, in the medieval cycle plays were performed. The *OED*'s description of its uncertain etymology suggests links to Latin and Greek roots that referred to a scaffold or framework, "a movable stage or scaffold used in theatres" (*OED*). By the early fifteenth century, as the performances of the mystery plays claimed a prominent place in the liturgical year, "pageant" referred not only to the platform stage, but also to the play performed on that stage.

Many now-obsolete uses of the word, such as "a performance intended to deceive; a trick," carry figurative meanings with pejorative implications. The notion that a pageant was an empty show likely contributed to the bias against viewing and reviewing pageants as a form of theatre, as did their ephemerality. In *The Tempest*, Prospero famously speaks of his "insubstantial pageant" (4.1.172). So suited to particular moments were some pageants that only rarely would they be performed at a different time or in a different place. Partly because of the ephemerality of a single performance or relatively short run, the lack of a published script or a celebrated author, many pageants were, until recently, only rarely the subject of scholarly analysis. Yet there are also uses of "pageant" with positive connotations to suggest an expansive sweep or comprehensive vision. The title of a standard US high school history textbook, *The American Pageant*, in print in seventeenth editions since 1956, uses "pageant" to entice its readers to study the past. Two short-lived journals used the title *Pageant* to suggest an affinity with the arts. One, edited by Gleeson White and Charles Hazelwood Shannon in London 1896–7, presented "British aestheticism to readers as an intellectual pursuit of art history, ancient myth, modern western culture, and decadent cosmopolitanism" (King 2019). The second, *The Pageant: A Magazine of Belles-Lettres*, published 1905–7 by Blue Sky Press in Chicago, was co-edited by Thomas Wood Stevens, the co-author of *The Pageant and Masque of Saint Louis* (1914). The specificity of the word also changed over time as did the nature of pageants.

An Enduring Idiom

World cultures have displayed a remarkable variety of spectacular drama involving personation that can be described as pageants. Since the time of the *trionfo* of Imperial Rome, cities and nations have used pageantry to legitimize, consolidate, and expand their power. Perhaps the pageants most often configured and studied as literature are the medieval religious pageants that flourished, especially in Northern Europe, from the fourteenth to the mid-sixteenth century. In producing the religious pageants of the medieval English mystery cycles, the guilds displayed their devotional piety and community engagement. The laity as well as the clergy now assumed responsibility for interpreting and propagating the Catholic faith. The guilds' pageants, moreover, inspired civic pride that was tethered to neither the Church nor the monarch. But by the mid-sixteenth century, the entire spectrum of the religious drama was proscribed as heretical and seditious.

In England, the medieval religious drama of earlier centuries was extinguished by 1600. As Roy Strong writes,

> Although by 1500 secular court festivals were much more prominent, the balance was still heavily in favour of religion and the Church. By 1600 that had changed. In countries that remained Catholic, ecclesiastical pomp in its new counter-reformation guise was to be complemented by what can only be called a liturgy of state which centered on the ruler. In the case of Protestant countries, there was not even a question of complement. It was one of total reversal. The liturgy of state ruthlessly replaced that of the medieval church.
>
> (1986: 19)

In Italy, the immense wealth and power of the Medici and Sforza courts transformed the pageant by shifting its focus from celebrating religious belief to celebrating themselves. Leonardo da Vinci's rise in Ludovico Sforza's Milan court came as a producer of pageants in the late fifteenth century: "as a spectacle-loving apprentice he had become enthralled by staging fantasies … there were many elements, both artistic and technical involved in producing such festivities, and all of them appealed to Leonardo: stage designs, costumes, scenery, music, mechanisms, choreography, allegorical allusions, automatons, and gadgets" (Isaacson 2018: 112).

By the mid-sixteenth century, many of the strategies, techniques, and dramaturgy of medieval religious pageants had been appropriated for purely secular spectacles; others, as ephemeral as Prospero's "insubstantial pageant," were lost or forgotten. Drama no longer venerated God. Pageants might still be performed in and by provincial towns to welcome the monarch, whereas masques were performed for the royal guest and the aristocracy. Of the many pageants staged during Queen Elizabeth's progresses in the late sixteenth century, Felicity Heal observes: "Their specific messages were various, but all worked within the ideal paradigm of the greatness of the honour accorded the host by the Queen's presence" (2007: 52). R. Malcolm Smuts points out that in London "there were no street pageants directly associated with reigning monarchs between 1559 and 1603, nor between 1606 and the Civil War" (2005: 66).

By the early seventeenth century, the word "pageant" had crossed from noun to verb and could mean "to display oneself." The reign of James I saw a proliferation of court spectacles that grew ever grander by employing, as did the Medici and Sforza courts, the creative talents and artistry of professional playwrights, musicians, designers, and technicians. With the suppression of the cycle plays, pageant-making was professionalized. Stephen Orgel notes that, "Renaissance festivals were the province of the greatest artists of the age; their number included Leonardo, Dürer, Mantegna, Holbein, Bronzino, Rubens, Buontalenti, Caron, Primaticcio, Callot, Monteverdi, Ferrabosco, Dowland, Campion, Lawes, Ronsard, Sidney, Jonson, and Milton" (1975: 41). Orgel asserts that royal entries, that of James I in particular, not only were performed for the monarch, but were "also, probably more significantly, a performance for the audience who footed the bill—in the case of civic pageantry, the guilds, city fathers, Inns of Court, foreign merchants or private magnates, for whom the production was an investment" (2011: 24). Although masques flourished at the Jacobean court, Gail Kern Paster writes that "because James disliked public shows far more than his politically canny predecessor, the number of civic pageants throughout England declines after his accession" (2011: 48). Pageants remained a regular feature of the Lord Mayor's Shows in London, which dated back to the twelfth century. Tracey Hill's landmark *Pageantry and Power* documents the diverse audiences that the Shows attracted. Produced by the City Livery Companies, the Shows' pageants were staged at sites of special import— the courtyard of St. Paul's, the conduits, and so on—but also played on pageant wagons, river barges, or temporary stages. Using mainly nonprofessional actors drawn from the livery companies but often written by established playwrights like Thomas Dekker, Thomas Heywood, Thomas Middleton, and Anthony Munday, they "resembled the court masques as well as the Shows' medieval predecessors" (Hill 2010: 150). Some of the Shows' pageants were published near the time of their performance and are, thanks to scholars like Bergeron and Hill, among the best understood.

Pageants are closely related to but can be differentiated from masques. Both are sensory spectacles that may involve a wide array of music and song, highly choreographed movement, elaborate costumes, sophisticated stage machinery, and special effects. Whereas pageants seek the very large, often communal audience, masques are typically entertainments for an elite. As such, the language of the pageants is often colloquial, accessible, and prosaic, while masques employ an elevated, poetic speech. Typically performed at court, masques use abstractions or allegorical figures to create, in Orgel's words, "heroic roles for the leaders of society" (1971: 367). Pageants targeted a much broader and less powerful audience in plainer, more familiar language. While masques tend to deify people and to portray abstract concepts, pageants can humanize the personages portrayed by showing them as inhabiting the spectator's world.

In the eighteenth century, political entities, especially emerging nation states, again sought out a wide spectrum of the population in public exercises to mark anniversaries, to commemorate their heroes and founders, and to instill national and civic pride. Following Benedict Anderson's seminal notion of "imagined communities," Jill Lepore, in *This America*, reminds us that "nation-states, when they form, imagine a past" (2019: 2). That past is not the past of earlier times. In many instances, the theatrical idiom used to disseminate a new history, especially of a new nation, was the pageant. In America, pageants developed with Independence. Under a carefully brokered arrangement, George Washington, who would not be president until 1789, entered newly liberated

New York City on November 25, 1783 only hours after British troops had departed. The city's population was ecstatic with excitement and celebration. Beginning the next year and "for generations after Evacuation Day of 1783, New Yorkers celebrated November 25 annually with parades, fireworks and pageants" (Axelrod 2006: 34). A few years later, a series of Federal Processions took place as individual states ratified the US Constitution in 1788. When New York became the tenth state to ratify, a grand festivity was planned for July 22, but was delayed by one day so that Jews of the city who celebrated Tishah B'Av could participate. The procession began on the morning of July 23, 1788 with "Columbus 'in ancient dress' on horseback," followed by representatives of trades and professions identified by "flags and banner ingeniously designed for the occasion" (Simpson 1925: 42–3). Amid the elaborately decorated floats was one bearing a near life-sized figure of George Washington. The highlight was the Federal Ship *Hamilton*, a miniature thirty-two-gun frigate (Figure 1).

When the 27-foot float bearing the ship reached the reviewing stand, her Pilot and Captain performed this dialogue:

Pilot   From whence came ye?

Capt. M   From the Old Constitution

Pilot   Where bound?

Capt. M   To the New Constitution.

(Simpson 1925: 46)

After a thirteen-gun salute (one for each state) and series of cheers, the ship was "moored" at the Bowling Green.[1] On another horse-drawn stage, "'the Federal Printing press' struck and distributed to the crowd several hundred copies of an ode and a song" to memorialize the event (Simpson 1925: 48). These pageants not only memorialized the very recent victory over the British and American Independence, but also channeled the intense elation of ordinary people. As a theatrical

Figure 1 *July 23, 1788: Federal ship* Hamilton *on a horse-drawn parade float in celebration of New York state's ratification of the Constitution. Photo by Fotosearch/Getty Images.*

form, pageants were ideally suited to personate the revolution's heroes and to create festive spectacles of community.

After the French Revolution, not only were the many rituals, rites, and ceremonies of the three Bourbon dynasties discarded, so also was the understanding of the past that had prevailed for the previous 200 years. Pageantry, however, did not die with Louis XVI. The festivals of the First French Republic that sprung up across France to transmit revolutionary culture "engaged enormous numbers of people in their dramatizations of shared patriotic enthusiasm" (Schama 1989: 502). In *Festivals and the French Revolution*, Mona Ozouf argues that the pageants of Jean-Louis David reconciled ordinary people to the new political order:

> In the clean-swept world that the Revolution seemed to offer the utopian dreamers, the suppression of hierarchies and the homogenization of the human condition left men alone. Men were individuals, in theory all identical, all

equal, but solitary. It was now the task of the legislator to connect them, a task that all the utopias of the [eighteenth] century took up with meticulous relish. ... The festival was an indispensable complement to the legislative system, for although the legislator makes laws for the people, festivals make people for the laws. (1994: 9)

Ozouf here argues that these pageants not only educated, but also transformed their performers and audiences.

In Ireland, the mass gatherings of Daniel O'Connell and his Repeal Association, known as monster meetings, demanded an end to the Penal Laws and Act of Union. In Gary Owens's formulation: "Every monster meeting was nothing less than a performance in three acts whose players and audiences shifted with each change of scenery" (1999: 247). O'Connell predicted that the astonishing turnout of 750,000 on Lady's Day, August 15, 1843, at the Hill of Tara would instill anger and fear in the British; it did precisely that. O'Connell's monster meetings were again banned as felonious treason. Unlike the hegemonic pageantry, this was demotic, counter-hegemonic pageantry performed by citizens who still did not have the vote, but by the 1840s had unprecedented mobility.

In the decades after the formation of the German Republic in 1871, waves of patriotic festivals and pageants swept across the new nation state. Matthew Jefferies documents the popularity of historical drama and historical pageants, especially ones concerning the *Gründerseit* ("the age of the founders"). For example, in 1884 for the 600th anniversary of the Pied Piper of Hamelin, "a large proportion of the town's inhabitants donned thirteenth century outfits" (2003: 188). Perhaps nowhere can the imperative to stage the nation's past in pageants be more clearly seen than in post-tsarist Russia. So vital were the pageants staged immediately after the Russian Revolution that a government agency, the Section for Mass Presentations and Spectacles, coordinated artists, architects, and playwrights, including Nikolai Evreinov, Konstantin Derzhavin, Anatoly Lunacharsky, and Alexei Gan.[2] In 1920, for the third anniversary of the October Revolution, thousands of people—trained ballet dancers and actors, circus performers, supernumeraries—participated in a reenactment, *The Storming of the Winter Palace*, in Petrograd. For the next seventy years, no one in what became the Soviet Union was unaware of the pageants, parades, and other public demonstrations that marked the "Octobers."

Mass meetings, often political in nature, were predicated on the mobility of tens of thousands made possible by the development of far-reaching networks of railways. In his three-volume paean to Richard Wagner, Louis Napoleon Parker, the most celebrated pageant-maker of the twentieth century, described Bayreuth as "almost inaccessible yet it stood in the very focus of the mid-European railway system, and could be made accessible enough on occasion" (1898: vol. 1, 34). No less essential than rail travel to the scale of these mass meetings were the development of photography and the proliferation of inexpensive newspapers. In the early twentieth century, even cheap newspapers could reproduce the photographs and illustrations that fed the appetite for pageantry in an increasingly vibrant visual culture. Walter Benjamin wrote of ways in which mechanical reproduction compromised and diminished works of fine art. Newspaper readers were now also viewers who consumed images of public spectacle just as insatiably as the mass-reproduced images and replicas of fine art. Extensive reporting, especially photographs, of these mass meetings quickened the participatory impulses of the public. The rich visual culture of the British suffrage movement produced not only exquisite banners, popular plays, revolutionary newspapers, and a material culture ranging from playing cards to fine jewelry, but also photo opportunities.

Unlike the United States and France in the eighteenth century and Germany in the nineteenth century, Britain was not a new nation state, but the passage of the Third Reform Act in 1884 remade Britain's electorate by increasing the number of registered voters threefold. For women and the disenfranchised Irish, pageants demonstrated their political consciousness and determination to have the vote. In the

United States, the pageant was the theatrical form of choice for progressives who saw an unprepared and undereducated electorate, including large numbers of immigrants. Throughout the English-speaking world, the heyday of civic pageants was intimately bound to the expansion of the franchise.

From the early nineteenth century, mass meetings in the UK, typically political in nature, attracted crowds and conditioned the public for participation in massive pageants: "In the early to middle decades of the nineteenth century, a slew of protest movements embraced the march as means to collective mobilization. Reformers walked" (Bryant et al. 2016: 11). People from all over the country could be rallied to celebrate or, more often, to protest. Especially after 1886, hegemonic displays attending royal visits and progresses triggered counter-hegemonic performances by Irish nationalists who answered the bombastic celebrations of power, a royal visit for instance, with gleefully subversive public displays of resistance. On the occasion of Queen Victoria's 1900 visit to Ireland, Inghinidhe na hÉireann (the Daughters of Erin) sponsored a Patriotic Children's Treat that paraded some 20,000 children through Dublin's streets (Condon 2000: 167–8). When Edward VII visited Dublin three years later, Maud Gonne hung her black petticoats out her window. On June 22, 1911, the Women's Coronation Procession, held five days before George V's coronation and in competition with *The Festival of Empire*, capitalized on the popularity of the term "pageant": there was a historical pageant, a pageant of empire, and a "prisoners' pageant." In the last of these, 700 women who had been arrested or jailed marched, not in shame, but in proud solidarity as a cohort.

"My Future is all in the Past"

In the late nineteenth century, the term "pageant" was no longer tethered to a theatrical form let alone a pageant wagon, but could refer to any ostentatious display. The resurgence of pageants as a theatrical idiom in Britain at the beginning of the twentieth century owed partly to Victoria's death on January 22, 1901. After the long, mournful viduity of his mother, Edward VII reveled in ceremony and spectacle. He had, said Lord Esher, the "curious power of visualising a pageant" (qtd. in Lacey 2002: 46). With the exception of the financial panic of 1907, Edward's reign (1905–11) was economically, militarily, and politically a relatively stable period not only in Britain but in North America and Western Europe as well. The South African Wars had ended. Britain had entered into the Entente Cordiale with France. Indeed, such stability may be requisite for pageants to flourish as they did in the years immediately before the First World War. The public, however, saw life-changing technological innovations during this period: private residences were electrified; the Ford Motor Company produced the Model T; the London Underground opened new tube lines; commercial aviation began. In art and literature, it was the age of modernism. Joyce had completed *Dubliners* and spent 1905–14 trying to get it published. Schoenberg's experiments in atonality date from this period. Cubism, futurism, and surrealism do as well.

Beginning in 1905, after Louis Napoleon Parker organized *The Sherborne Pageant*, "pageant" more often referred specifically to a local historical pageant. Trained at the Royal Academy of Music in London, Parker composed numerous songs and cantatas while in his twenties and thirties and by his fortieth birthday had had several plays performed both in the West End and on Broadway. Many of his plays were translations or adaptations of works by Rostand, Hermann Sudermann, or Dickens. Parker's fluency in many languages first attracted him to dramatic adaptation, an experience he found as useful as his musical background, in creating pageants. *The Sherborne Pageant* incorporated music, song, dance, and his narrative in a very successful spectacle that selectively portrayed the history of a Dorset village between 705 and 1593. *The Sherborne Pageant* was so well received that it begot five other town pageants by "pageant-master" Parker and scores of historical pageants in and beyond Britain. When interviewed by the *New York Times* during the successful Broadway run of his play *Pomander Walk* in 1911, Parker reflected on his career: "You want the story of my past and my plans for the future? ... My future is all in the past."[3]

The pageants that flourished in the English-speaking world after 1905 typically staged a sequence of historical episodes. Historical pageants of this period routinely claimed authenticity and accuracy in even the smallest archaeological detail of costume, armaments, and implements and engaged artists and artisans to create colorful displays in familiar vernacular forms. Parker's historical pageants used thousands of unpaid, local amateurs to depict successive episodes from a community's history arranged chronologically in an outdoor venue. Three of these features—a chronological episodic structure, outdoor venue, and engagement of local people (typically amateur rather than professional actors and practitioners)—offer continuities reaching back to the medieval mystery cycles and forward to contemporary pageants. But the focus of these historical pageants was plainly secular, even though religious figures might appear. Several historical pageants advertised themselves as commemorating a historical event; they all aimed to create a vast panoply of the past. Whereas commemoration targets a specific individual or date, historical pageantry sweeps through decades, centuries, even millennia. And whereas commemoration is often contentious and almost inevitably solemn, historical pageantry is festive, celebratory, even carnivalesque.

Parker's town pageants offered a theatrical bricolage of history, spectacle, music, and audience participation to provide access to the community's heritage. They were greeted with widespread praise. Typical of the enthusiasm for his pageants is the response of *The Manchester Guardian* on July 16, 1907:

> The pageant is the latest and most picturesque development of civic life. One may fairly claim it as a manifestation of all that is best in the new democracy, made possible by the

broadening and refining of influences of popular education, and successful only as far as it is able to command the aid of all classes of society in the task of setting forth those great deeds of old days which have made our cities what they are. (qtd. in Vandrei 2018: 190)

Under these conditions in Britain, historical pageants took root and thrived until Britain entered the First World War.

Modernist and Anti-modernist

Parker was repelled by modern life. He was horrified when,

confronted with the latest steel-frame six or seven storied Emporium, the basement of which is all plate-glass and ginger bread, covered with horrible advertisements of monstrous comestibles, quack nostrums, foods for the fat, pale pills for pink people, all labeled with hideous outrages on the English language in the shape of new words— clenol for a soap, quicklite for a match, ritefast for an ink. (1905: 145)

As Meghan Lau observes, "With the work of John Ruskin, William Morris, and others in mind, Parker envisioned the pageant as temporarily stemming the tide of industrialism" (2011: 271).

In America, too, pageant-makers warned of the pernicious intrusion of mechanized technologies into daily life and saw pageants as a theatrical form to restore happiness and joy. Ralph Davol even argued for pageants as a form of fine art. "Pageantry," he wrote, "is founded on the deep, sane, human instinct of happiness. So long as man made things by hand he found joy in his work. The machine crushes this joy and he seeks elsewhere for happiness … [pageants] restore and preserve the picturesque side of life which has been grievously marred by most of our modern mechanical devices" (1914b: 299–301). The profound anxieties of twentieth-century life that inform pageants on both sides of the Atlantic resist all that is modern by seeking refuge in the distant past, but it is precisely also what Hobsbawm described as characteristic of the modern, the propensity for "the invention of tradition." For Hobsbawm, tradition is "a set of practices, normally governed by overtly or tacitly accepted rules and of a ritual or of a symbolic nature, which seek to inculcate certain values and norms in behavior by repetition, which automatically implies continuity with the past" (1983: 1), that, he points out, is "largely factitious" (2). Traditions, he argued, are invented at moments of profound cultural change, especially when "modern nations and all their impedimenta generally claim to be the opposite of novel, namely rooted in the remotest antiquity, and the opposite of constructed" (13). From the very different perspectives of Hobsbawm and Parker, historical pageants are simultaneously anti-modern and modern.

Beyond the invention of tradition, there are other senses in which these historical pageants can be construed as modern. Parker routinely spoke of his pageants as innovative, a new form of drama, a claim that was routinely and unquestioningly repeated in the press. His six town pageants clearly do project an alternative reading of place by celebrating a community usually overlooked or dismissed as inconsequential. On one level, his pageants reject the elite, the professional, the expert in favor of the local, the homespun, the communal. They do not see historical personages or events as remote, but immediate corporeal realities. Because they involve large numbers of amateur performers, they speak to and of an increasingly democratic world that by the time of *Isles of Wonder* in 2012 would be "for everyone."

Paul Readman cautions against dismissing the historical pageants as naïve exercises foisted upon the British (as well as Irish and American) people. The pageant movement, he argues, "is probably best understood outside the 'invention of tradition' paradigm: far from being an artificial imposture, mediated through ritualized ceremony at the behest of the ruling classes, public engagement with the past was genuine and deep-rooted" (2005: 150). Readman underscores the growing interest in the past evident in the study of history, in antiquarianism and much more widely in the literary and visual arts in the late nineteenth and early twentieth centuries. Reginald Blunt, for instance, had been writing about his home borough for many years before he published *An Illustrated Historical Handbook of the Parish of Chelsea* in 1900, and that was eight years before he contributed to the *Chelsea Historical Pageant*. By the 1880s, the appearance of historical tableaux and pageants in processions was not uncommon. For the 1888 tercentenary of the defeat of the Spanish Armada, a pageant in Plymouth "celebrated characters of the Elizabethan and Victorian eras [and] historical tableaux representing all the sovereigns of England from William the Conqueror to her Majesty the Queen [Victoria]."[4] For *The Pageant at Fountains Abbey* in 1896 in Ripon, "there were 500 persons, in appropriate costume, depicting the usages and characteristics of every period of our [English] history" from Boadicea to Victoria.[5] Joseph McBrinn details the procession, banners, exhibits, arts and crafts that drew 5,000 to another of Francis Joseph Bigger's pageants of Ulster's history and heritage, the Feis na nGleann (Festival of the Nine Glens in Antrim and Rathlin Island) on June 30, 1904. By this date, a year before Parker's first town pageant, Bigger had been orchestrating the talents of artists, musicians, and theatre practitioners such as Jack Morrow, John Patrick Campbell, and Alice Milligan to create conspicuously public pageants of Ulster's identity for nearly a decade.

"The Redemption of Leisure"

In the United States, the high priest of American pageantry, Percy MacKaye (1875–1956), argued that there were three kinds of theatre: classical drama, vaudeville, and pageants. He wrote and advocated for the last of these as "the drama of democracy." Some in the American pageant movement responded to the waves of immigrants and sought to represent the American past to an ever-expanding electorate. Immigration to the United States peaked in 1907; its 13.5 million immigrants comprised 14.6 percent of the 92,228,496 enumerated in the 1910 US census. As during other periods and in other places, pageants could introduce recently enfranchised voters to their political choices and responsibilities. In his *The New Citizenship: A Civic Ritual Devised for Places of Public Meeting in America*, Percy MacKaye hoped "to create an appropriate national ritual of American Citizenship" (1915: 5) specifically for use at naturalization ceremonies to distill the democratic ideals of American government and history for new citizens. His pageant of citizenship featured Liberty (a man), America (a woman), representatives of the (then) forty-eight states, the thirteen original colonies, fifty-six signers of the Declaration of Independence, Alexander Hamilton, Benjamin Franklin, George Washington, Thomas Jefferson, Abraham Lincoln, and scores of "new citizens" (25). At the end of his pageant, Liberty exhorts the audience: "Citizens! You who came to my altar as separate groups depart now as a community of Americans; you who came lonely and individual go forth in the fellowship of a common will—the will for justice and freedom" (86). No longer is the audience distinct from the other Americans on stage; they are one. MacKaye's appendix to *The New Citizenship* revealed the deep anxieties over immigration that pageants might assuage: the 1910 census shows that "there are at the very least 3,000,000 unnaturalized males over 21 years of age in the United States … Since 1910 more than 5,000,000 immigrants have been added to the population of the United States" (91). MacKaye had not even reckoned with women's suffrage, but he realized both the importance of developing civic rituals and the emotive power of naturalization ceremonies. MacKaye's deep anxieties over immigration were tied to his interest in eugenics, mostly clearly seen in his play *To-morrow*.[6] His "positive eugenics" (1912b: vii) also inform a "community masque" he crafted for the Shakespeare tercentennial, *Caliban by the Yellow Sands* (1916).

With other American progressives, Percy MacKaye advocated for state support of pageants in the form of dedicated sites and subsidized performances to lift people out of the misery of the modern. To him, pageants offered nothing less than "the redemption of leisure" (1912a), with the implication that leisure had fallen into myriad wasteful, if not disreputable, usages: yellow journalism, sensational fiction, and cheap kitsch at one end of that spectrum; drunkenness, rowdyism, and criminality at the other. In Glassberg's analysis "MacKaye's politics, like his symbolic theatre, was full of idealistic abstraction—that an enlightened public inspired by men and women governing according to the loftiest principles could bloodlessly transform the harsh realities of modern industrialism into something more aesthetically pleasing fair, and humane" (1990: 171). So fervent was the American interest in pageants that William Chauncy Langdon (1877–1947), Hazel MacKaye (Percy's sister, 1880–1944), and others organized the American Pageant Association (APA). Founded in 1913, the APA sought both to promote and to regulate the performance of pageants. In the *APA Bulletin*, Mary Porter Beegle distinguished two kinds of pageants: the commercial and the community, or true, pageant. The latter was "a new and possible art for the people, of which the final aim is Social Service. Social Service, taken in its broadest sense, means bringing to the people the opportunity to organize, co-operate and unite in a form of art production readily accessible to all."[7]

The American pageant movement found more traction and advocates in the Northeast and Midwest than elsewhere in the United States. Many pageant proponents were academics.[8] Robert Withington was both an advocate and an academic. Before Withington became a literary historian, he was a disciple of Parker, an enthusiast in American community pageantry, and the author of his own *A Manual of Pageantry* (1915).[9]

In service to the pageant movement, his two-volume *English Pageantry: An Historical Outline* (1918 and 1920) catalogued paratheatrical performances beginning with folk mumming and moving chronologically through centuries of British exemplars until he reached the apotheosis, the "Parkerian Pageant" of his own day.

On June 7, 1913, *The Pageant of the Paterson Strike* interrupted the momentum of the American movement. The Paterson strike, which began on February 25, 1913, demanded an eight-hour workday for workers in a New Jersey silk factory. Sympathetic New Yorkers including John Read, Walter Lippman, and Robert Edmond Jones (who designed the poster) and John Sloan (who designed the backdrop depicting the Paterson mills) capitalized on the popularity of the genre to create a counter-hegemonic pageant. Under the auspices of the Industrial Workers of the World (the "Wobblies"), the pageant was created by intellectuals and artists, but performed "by the strikers themselves." On that June afternoon, 900 men traveled from Paterson by train to Manhattan and paraded up Fifth Avenue to Madison Square Garden. The pageant's six episodes began with a depiction of "the mills alive—the workers dead" and moved through the workers' picketing, a reenactment of the funeral of Vincenzo (or Valentino) Modestino, choral interludes, the strikers' children being taken from their parents, and finally a strike meeting with fiery orations. Here, as in the 1911 Pageant of Women's Trades and Professions, the workers performed as themselves. Martin Green calls particular attention to the staging of *The Pageant of the Paterson Strike*, among the first of many labor pageants to come, in which the performers moved through the audience in Madison Square Garden, effacing any barrier between them: "actors and audience were of one class and one hope" (1989: 204).

So powerful was the impact of *The Pageant of the Paterson Strike* that the APA's focus moved away from town pageants and toward the celebration of Shakespeare's tercentennial in 1915 and 1916. *The Pageant of the Paterson Strike* may also have diverted the mainstream of American pageants away from local history and toward edifying but more abstract themes. A strain of nature pageants, such as Percy MacKaye's *Sanctuary: A Bird Masque* (1913), appeared in the second decade of the twentieth century, as did peace pageants that opposed American entry into the First World War. American entry in the war on April 6, 1917 brought a flurry of patriotic pageants in support of the war effort. Typical is Thomas Wood Stevens's *The Drawing of the Sword*, which was directed by Ben Iden Payne at the Carnegie Institute of Technology in Pittsburgh and later at the Chautauqua Institution. Progressives were also keen to channel the festivities around the Fourth of July away from vulgar, loutish displays and toward respectful patriotism. Langdon's *Celebration of the Fourth of July by Means of Pageantry*, for instance, wrote of "the revulsion against the suffering incident to the old celebrations" (1912: 4) and provided templates for salutary community pageants to celebrate Independence Day.

The handbooks for pageant production that proliferated in the United States track the evolving uses of the genre. Esther Willard Bates's *Pageants and Pageantry* (1912) was introduced by William Orr, Deputy Commissioner of Education in Massachusetts, who recommended pageant productions by high school students. In *Historical Pageantry: A Treatise and a Bibliography* (1916), Ethel T. Rockwell embraced the Parkerian model and the progressive agenda: "the art of historical pageantry has served to demonstrate the idealism of our American democracy, and has satisfied the popular passion for art" (1916: 5). Caroline Hill Davis's *Pageants in Great Britain and the United States* (1916) documented the spread and diversification of the movement in the UK and the United States. By 1923, *A Guide to Religious Pageantry* by Mason Crum, Professor of Religious Education in Columbia College, pointed to the enduring attraction to celebrating Christian holidays with pageants, usually performed by children.

After the First World War, pageants, especially in the UK, diversified in several directions. Established literary figures like T. S. Eliot and E. M. Forster wrote pageants. Eliot's *The*

Rock: A Pageant Play was performed at Sadler's Wells Theatre in 1934 to benefit a church-building fund. The Redress of the Past website describes *The Abinger Pageant* as "probably the most written-about pageant due to the two figures behind its creation, E. M. Forster and Ralph Vaughan Williams."[10] Forster and Williams also collaborated on *England's Pleasant Land* (1938). Virginia Woolf's novel *Between the Acts* (1939) cast a very cold eye on village pageants.

Historical pageants proved attractive in the many civic weeks, especially in Manchester and Liverpool, in the late 1920s and 1930s, not least because they shared nearly identical goals. Tom Hulme points out that the 1924 British Empire Exhibition "inaugurated the first Civic Weeks in Britain, which then spread rapidly across the north and Midlands. Civic Weeks were associated with entertainment, and historical pageants especially" (2017: 273). Here, too, pageants proved an appealing vehicle for civic pride. More than 100,000 are reported to have attended the historical pageant held during Manchester's 1926 Civic Week (Wildman 2016: 72).

Perhaps drawing inspiration from *The Pageant of the Paterson Strike* or the Soviet Union's Octobers, labor movements in both the UK and the United States also turned to pageants. Mick Wallis surveys a series of British labor pageants, some read in reaction against civic week pageants, sponsored by the Co-operative Society and the Communist Party in the mid-to-late 1930s (Wallis 1994, 1995). [11] In the United States, the prolific journalist, screenwriter, and playwright Ben Hecht wrote a number of pageants: some labor pageants; others advocated for American entry into the Second World War or supported the war effort; finally, one exposed the Nazi genocide of the Jews. Shortly before the United States entered the Second World War, Hecht and Charles MacArthur, his collaborator on *The Front Page* (play, 1928; film, 1931), created a pageant, *Fun to Be Free*, promoting US intervention in the war in Europe. Garrett Eisler describes their October 1941 pageant as containing "reverential enactments of such iconic scenes from American history as the signing of the Declaration of Independence and

Lincoln's Gettysburg address ... [but] reframing these familiar scenes as conflicts between militant liberalism and corrupt 'appeasement'" (2016: 199). Eight months later, Hecht created a *Labor for Victory* radio pageant in support of the American war effort that was broadcast nationwide by NBC radio on May 30, 1942 and published on June 2, 1942 as *Pageant of American Labor* by the newspaper of the American Federation of Labor. In 1943, Hecht hoped that by exposing the Nazi death camps in *We Will Never Die*, he would bring greater urgency to the American engagement in the war in Europe. At this early date, Hecht even named Treblinka as one of "the extermination camps."[12] In collaboration with Kurt Weill, Moss Hart, Billy Rose, and Ernest Lubitsch, he assembled an all-star cast that included John Garfield, Edward G. Robinson, and Sylvia Sydney. Produced at first in Madison Square Garden in New York City and then at the Hollywood Bowl, it was seen by more than 100,000; broadcast on national radio in America, it was heard by millions. The wider circulation of *We Will Never Die* was suppressed (see Skloot 1985; Whitfield 1996), but the theatrical qualities of Hecht's pageants were nearly extinguished by radio broadcast. Ultimately, *We Will Never Die* failed to galvanize Americans or alter American policy.

Today, some local pageants that involve historical personation are the focal point of celebrations that center on the claim, however dubious, not only of authenticity, but also of historical uniqueness. Since 1445, the women of Olney, Buckinghamshire, claim to have annually staged a pancake race on Shrove Tuesday. Even when wearing Nikes, today's performers acknowledge the medieval origins of the event by costuming themselves in headscarf and apron. In the New World, residents of Tampa, Florida, have celebrated a Gasparilla Pirate Festival since 1904. Those in Punxsutawney, Pennsylvania, festively gather every February 2 for an ocular groundhog to forecast the continuation or end of winter.

In 1990, two academic studies of early twentieth-century pageants, one by a choreographer and the other by a historian, documented the immense popularity of historical pageants

in the United States. The choreographer and dance historian
Naima Prevots offered the now-surprising assertion that
"pageantry was a major influence in shaping American theatre"
(1990: 105). She refers, however, principally to pageantry's
influence on the Little Theatre Movement as transmitted by
academics like George Pierce Baker (1866–1935) and Frederick
H. Koch (1877–1944) in the period before 1930. The historian
David Glassberg, in *American Historical Pageantry: The Uses
of Tradition in the Early Twentieth Century*, examines US
pageants as public history, as "part of the larger, essentially
untold history of popular images and uses of tradition in
America" (1990: 1). Glassberg argues that "one use of history
was unique to pageantry and to the early twentieth century:
the belief that history could be made into a dramatic public
ritual through which the resident of a town, by acting out the
right version of their past, could bring about some kind of
future social and political transformation" (4).

Several theatre theoreticians point to the theatrical elements
at work in pageants, but often turn away from populist
spectacles and instead incline toward elite, metropolitan
experiments. Richard Schechner's interrogation of "large-
scale performative events that cannot be easily classified as
belonging to either ritual or theatre or politics" (1994: 4)
leads him to the American and European avant-garde and
to distant, exotic cultures. Several scholars have explored
the influence of Wagner's *Gesamtkunstwerk* (the total work
of art) on playwrights like Paul Claudel or Antonin Artaud
or the European avant-garde. Roland Barthes's definition
of theatricality as "theater-minus-text" (1972: 25) similarly
beckons theatre historians to engage with pageants. One of
the richest veins of commentary on pageants comes from
anthropologists and ethnographers like Victor Turner who
explored "the anthropology of performance," the links between
ritual and theatre. Turner's writings on "*communitas*," when
audiences and participants feel united in an organic, spiritual
sense, has particular relevance to pageants. Erika Fischer-
Lichte, the most illuminating theatre scholar to consider

pageants, examines the "re-theatricalization of theatre" (1997: 72 *passim*) in a wide range of paratheatrical forms.

Pageants, especially twentieth-century historical pageants, have been justly criticized for their selectivity, ahistoricity, conservatism, and willingness to sanitize and to glorify the past. Patrick Wright's critique of the English heritage industry argues that,

> what much of utopianism has alluded to or postulated as the challenge of history—something that needs to be brought about—ends up behind us, already accomplished and ready for exhibition as "the past". Where there was active historicity there is now decoration and display; in the place of memory, amnesia swaggers out in historical fancy dress. (1985: 74)

Following Wright, Jed Esty writes,

> the typical pageant managed to represent hundreds of years of English history by suggesting that all important things had stayed the same. The key to the genre, then, is that it displays a series of chronological episodes in order to project the absence of change. The pageant-play dissolves history into the seductive symbolic continuity of rural folk-ways and national traditions. (2009: 59)

For Wright and Esty, the pernicious quality of historical pageants lies in the narcotic nostalgia that diverts people from either present action or an honest engagement with the past. Similarly, the grand scale of pageants troubles contemporary commentators. In discussing the first Festival of the Federation, Simon Schama touches on this suspicion of pageants:

> It is difficult, in the twentieth century, to sympathize with these mass demonstrations of fraternal togetherness. We have seen too much orchestrated banner waving—great field of arms harvested in ecstatic solidarity—heard too much

chanting in unison to avoid either cynicism or suspicion. But however jejune the experience, there is no question that it was intensely felt by participants as a way of turning inner fears into outward elation, of covering the dismaying sense of recklessness stirred by revolutionary newness with a great cloak of solidarity. (1989: 503–4)

By the 1930s, such participatory public spectacles assumed deeply menacing dimensions when the Third Reich replaced the Weimar Republic.

On the other hand, public theatre has strong enthusiasts today who argue, much as did Percy MacKaye, for state support of various paratheatrical forms, including pageants. Pageants play a lucrative part in tourist initiatives. *The New Founde Trinity Pageant* has helped to sustain tourism to the tiny (pop. 169) town of Trinity, Newfoundland, since 1993. Street theatre companies like Royal de Luxe and Générik Vapeur in France and Dogtroep in the Netherlands continue to transgress dramatic conventions in their public pageants. The Galway-based Macnas company, now in its fourth decade, still fulfills its original statement by designing "opportunities for celebration and ritual through spectacles with the community."[13]

1

The Middle English Noah Pageants

The hegemonic Christianity of medieval Europe offered the faithful a spectrum of theatrical and theatre-like experiences through the celebration of the Mass and of holy days, saints days, and holidays. T. P. Dolan catalogues the elements of the Catholic Mass that mark it, even when celebrated in Latin, as theatrical: ritual movements, distinctive clothing, precious accoutrements, music and song, the ringing of bells, the burning of incense, a well-defined relationship between the celebrant and the laity, and the congregation's "participation in the dialogue at certain stages of the Liturgy" (2005: 22). Especially in cathedral towns, artisans working in stone, precious metals, fabric, and stained or painted glass created powerful sensory experiences for the faithful. In the sacred space of the church, where natural light was architecturally managed by stone masons who aimed to build a new Jerusalem, all of the senses could be engaged, even if (perhaps because) the vernacular was not in use. The very appetite for spectacle may have been an expression of piety.

Of the range and variety of "dramatic activity" that pervaded Europe in the fourteenth and fifteenth centuries, Lynette R. Muir writes:

> flourishing and varied dramatic activity in towns and villages [occurred] all over Europe. Religious subjects make

up the greater part of the surviving repertory and dominate
the records. They were performed in churches and palaces,
streets, squares and graveyards. They might be staged in a
single (often indoor) location; in a processional or stational
model or on a multiple fixed-location set. (1997: 45)

Eamon Duffy points to the increasing literacy, even among
women, as "the crucial factor in the growth of a well-instructed
laity in fifteenth-century England" (2006: 68). In consequence,
the circulation of religious texts "brought religious instruction
out of the church, into the household and the gildhall and
thereby into direct competition with secular entertainment"
(69). From the thirteenth century, many northern European
cities and towns used pageants to impart a knowledge of the
tenets of Christian faith to a population that overwhelmingly
lacked formal schooling.

From the twelfth century, medieval Christian drama
developed in several directions. The most common
classifications differentiate liturgical plays, mystery cycles,
moralities, and miracle plays. Alexandra F. Johnston, however,
points out that "the biblical plays were part of the intricate
cultural tapestry of the liturgy, the non-dramatic literature, the
art and the ceremony of late medieval England" (2017: 187).
These theatrical and para-theatrical forms held the potential
for spectacle, and pageants were at the heart of many of these.
Miracle plays, for instance, present arresting episodes from
the lives of St. Ursula, St. George, or Mary Magdalene. Of the
Digby *Mary Magdalene*, Theresa Coletti observes:

The play *is* remarkably spectacular, providing for regular
journeying of human and divine messengers, sudden
appearances and disappearances of Jesus on earth and in
heaven, a cloud that descends from heaven to set a pagan
temple on fire, seven devils that "dewoyde" from Mary
during the feast at the home of Simon the Pharisee, a
floating ship that crosses the platea with saintly and regal
cargo, visionary processions of Mary and angels scripted

by Jesus, and the saint's elevation into the clouds for her
daily feedings with heavenly manna. (2004: 25, emphasis
in original)

Although Coletti's focus is on other aspects of medieval
religious drama, the spectacular dimension certainly allies the
Digby *Mary Magdalene* with pageants new and old.

The mystery plays were performed over a period of about
two centuries, from the late fourteenth until the late sixteenth
century, and have had a vibrant afterlife in the twentieth and
into the twenty-first centuries. The exact origins of the mystery
cycles in England remain contested. Martin Stevens, for
example, argues that a parade of tableaux vivants through the
streets of York evolved into the stational mode for pageants.
Hardin Craig describes the emergence of the mystery cycles
as "the union of pre-existent plays and groups of plays into
vast cyclic combinations, extensive in scope, conventional in
contents, long familiar to the people, and, for the most part,
of native growth" (1955: 138). Other scholars advance a "big
bang" theory, but by 1377, the cycle of the York mystery
plays was well established. The extant texts and records
have been, especially in the past seventy years, the subject
of intense scholarship and revision. Some scholars argue
that the designation of the cycles as Corpus Christi plays is
a misnomer because they were frequently performed around
Whitsun (Pentecost) during a festive period lasting several
days rather than on a single day. No longer are the plays of the
Towneley cycle associated primarily let alone exclusively with
Wakefield. Much that is known about the medieval mystery
cycles remains provisional, qualified, or speculative because a
continuous revision takes place as scholarship discloses new
records, accounts, and images.

The four English mystery cycles—Chester, N-Town,
Towneley, and York—are the best known because these are
the manuscripts that have survived, but others, now lost,
certainly existed. In some instances, the texts that survive may
never have been performed. The cycles are associated with

prosperous market towns and cathedral cities clustered in the Midlands (i.e., outside of London) with the wealth, stability, and cohesion needed to undertake their demanding, spectacular performance. The fifteenth century in England was marked not only by natural disruptions such as plague and drought, but also by thirty years (1455–85) of civil war. Nonetheless, these specific towns enjoyed the sustained periods of prosperity and continuity that seem prerequisite for public pageantry to thrive. Johnston, for instances, asserts that, after the War of the Roses, at the end of the fifteenth century "there must have been a stable community within York" (2017: 189).

The largest group of plays to survive comprises the York cycle, whose forty-eight extant plays show "an extraordinary variety of dramatic and poetic styles. ... a number of the pageants can be shown to date from different periods, or to have been replaced by new (but unrecorded) versions during the later life of the cycle, or to have been dropped from production altogether" (Beadle 2008: 103). The twenty-three plays in the Chester cycle, which were, by 1531/2, performed in the days following Whitsun (Mills 2008: 134), include an Expositor (or Crier), an authoritative voice (absent, however, from the Noah episode). The N-Town (as in Name-goes-here) cycle, associated with the East Midlands, contains forty-two episodes, which likely made use of both pageant wagons and scaffolds (fixed raised stages). The thirty-two plays that make up the extant Towneley cycle, whose distinctive Wakefield stanza form still employs the cycle's earlier name, are remarkable for their humor and psychologically robust characters.

The episodic structure of the mystery cycles demanded relatively short pageants, usually under 500 lines, that could be performed in about fifteen to thirty minutes. Individual episodes typically have a singular, well-defined action that might suggest Aristotle's unity of action, but they use a sophisticated typology that makes implicit comparisons with other pageants in the cycle and may allude to contemporary events. A single pageant could both echo and foreshadow other episodes, thus giving unity to the complete cycle. Although musicians and actors playing central roles were sometimes paid, most of the mystery cycle performers were amateurs. The short duration of individual pageants is intimately connected to their performance by amateurs. Rhyme and highly alliterative language facilitated the memorization by nonprofessionals. Whereas the clergy celebrated the earliest liturgical drama, the laity performed the great mystery cycles.

The mystery cycles were governed by both secular and religious authorities. The Church exerted control over the subject matter and dialogue and was sometimes responsible for the preservation of texts of the pageants themselves. The laity, specifically the guilds, rather than clerics, undertook the production of the cycle plays, and did so gladly, partially as a matter of civic pride. The pageants demonstrated the guilds' prosperity, power, and importance as well as their piety.

Medieval guilds initially brought together local merchants, artisans, or craftsmen engaged in a specific profession not to perform pageants, but to better their members, to promote their profession, and to regulate employment, trade, and training. By the early fifteenth century, some guilds, such as the Mercers, were wealthy and, consequently, powerful. The common pattern was that specific pageants were assigned to individual guilds; a guild is often said to have ownership of a specific play, and for a very long period, possibly more than a century. There was a commonsense at work in assigning the pageants to specific guilds: the Bakers in York presented the Last Supper; the Butchers in York, the Death of Christ; the Iron-mongers in Chester, the Crucifixion. In some instances, the pageant offered the guild an opportunity to display its skills: baking the bread, making the nails, building the ship. In York and Newcastle, the Shipwrights staged the construction of the ark; in Chester, it was the Waterleaders and Drawers of the Dee.

In performing the cycle plays, the guilds navigated between secular and religious functions and negotiated among existing ecclesiastical, aristocratic, and civic power structures. With specific reference to the N-Town pageants, Janette Dillon writes that "the likely setting is a major public event, bringing the religious and secular parts of the community together in a celebration of their interaction and interdependence" (1998: 32). The episodes they performed were expressly religious and subject to both clerical and civic control, but the guilds assumed or wrested a large measure of control over the performance of the plays. Duffy and others underscore the vital importance of the guilds' pageants because they conveyed religious instruction not in Latin, the language of the clergy, but in the vernacular. Whereas the earliest liturgical drama was, like the Mass, in Latin, with the exception of a few familiar Latin phrases and even fewer instances of French, the mystery plays were performed in the vernacular, Middle English.[1]

As the cycles flourished, civic laws mandated the conditions of the guilds' presentation of their assigned pageants. Chambers (1903: vol. 2, 110) notes that local statues set out criteria for the guilds' performance of pageants; other laws stipulated fines for guild members who would be away or did not participate in the pageant. Chambers also details the guilds' many responsibilities for pageant production:

> At Coventry, where the burden upon the crafts [guilds] was perhaps heaviest, they were responsible for the provision, repairing, ornamenting, cleaning, and strewing with rushes of the pageant [wagons], for the "ferme" or rent of the pageant house, for the payment of actors, minstrels, and prompter, for the revision of the play-book and songs and the copying of parts, for costumes and properties, and above all for the copious refreshment before and after the play, at the stations, and during the preliminary rehearsals. (115–16)

The pageants came to demand a wide range of theatrical skills and talents from members of the laity who were not theatre professionals. In "The Doomsday Pageant of the York Mercers, 1433," Johnston and Margaret Dorrell detailed the elaborate pageant wagon and the extensive inventory of stage properties and costumes for what was likely the most lavish pageant in the York cycle.

As the cycles evolved and expanded, further economic factors came into play. The medieval cycles became attractions that drew pilgrim-like spectators from beyond the city or town. Of the York cycle, the seventeenth-century antiquarian William Dugdale wrote of "the confluence of people from farr and neare to see that shew was extraordinary great, and yielded now small advantage to this cittye" (qtd. in Chambers 1903: vol. 2, 110). The flood of visitors, which in about 1392 included Richard II, and the influx of cash into the local economy may well have contributed to the guilds' and the communities' enthusiasm for the pageants, a phenomenon that anticipates the staging of pageants as part of a tourist initiative.

Perhaps more important, the same guild performed the same episode year after year and over decades, which had implications for both the performers and the audiences. The circumstances of the guilds' production of the cycle plays make them unlike many other pageants, which were performed only once or in a short run of multiple performances and, hence, did not allow for revision and the gradual accretion of effective theatrical elements. For an individual guild, repetition would develop certain practices and routines so that their staging of their pageant naturally evolved. There was an inevitable refinement and accretion of effective elements of stagecraft: costumes, blocking, props, music, song, and sound and scenic effects. Moreover, all that created the pageant's *mise en scène*, especially the construction of the ark, was held in an institutional memory by members of the guild. Audiences, too, would recall and then look forward to specific episodes, such as the Chester episode of "The Magi and Herod." When Hamlet cautions the Players against "o'erdoing Termagant; it out-Herods Herod" (3.2.14–15), he recalls the histrionics associated with Herod's tirades as performed by the Vintners. The most effective, impactful features of their production would be amplified, expanded, augmented—a growth that might elude the surviving textual evidence. The pageants were both entertainment and instruction, and as such they imbricated secular pleasures and religious piety.

In medieval England, families typically practiced the same craft or profession from generation to generation over decades, even centuries. By the fifteenth century, people presenting the Noah episode might have grown up with it from the earliest years of childhood through their apprenticeship in the guild to their position of responsibility for presenting the pageant. Even though the guild members were amateurs, many would have developed strong senses of effective stagecraft and theatricality. At least to some degree, the ambition to surpass expectations, to produce ever-better pageants motivated a sense of competition among guilds; the pageants would have evolved to become more effective in their staging, more engaging to their audiences, and more flattering to their guild. Enthusiasm for pageant production may well have waxed and waned over the long life of the cycles, but strong lines of continuity were likely year after year.

In realizing these events on stage and in familiar surroundings, the cycles could teach and then amplify Christian beliefs by inviting the audience to experience them as physical realities rather than remote tales or abstractions. This is a predictable and recurrent function of pageants, whether they intend to intensify the audience's religious faith, its political beliefs, or its heritage. Centuries later, at the beginning of the twentieth century, pageants became a vehicle to instill civic pride or inform new voters. Pageants are especially effective in this regard because their stagecraft is overtly theatrical in appealing to all the senses. Given that the cycles were performed regularly if not annually and over several generations, even the earliest audiences brought a shared cultural literacy, some sense of these biblical characters and events to the productions. As Janet Hill notes: "everyone in the audience was familiar with the Bible stories: they knew the story of Noah well—who was saved, who was not; they knew that Eden was a fruitful garden; they were aware that soldiers crucified Christ and that at the last supper Christ broke bread and drank wine" (2002: 25). The mystery cycles aspired to educate their audiences, to provide human detail by fleshing out the rudimentary knowledge that audiences may have brought to the performance with sometimes visceral spectacle.

Some critics point to a narrowly didactic purpose for the medieval pageants as "unashamedly informative, didactic productions" (Walker 2008: 79). Indeed, medieval morality plays such as *Everyman* (*c*.1510) used allegorical figures to warn of the worldly snares that stood in the way of salvation. In the case of the Noah plays, Unger bluntly argues they show "how bad behavior was punished" (1992: 112). But whereas individual episodes might offer a simple moral, it was framed by and in turn contributed to a *grand récit* of human salvation, a master narrative of Christianity performed by the laity. Especially as performed annually, the pageants offered audiences the potential to progress from simply knowing the story of Noah to understanding its implications and even to intellectualizing its typology, all while responding emotionally to an inventively staged production in a festive environment.

The cycles were often, but not exclusively, staged on the Feast of Corpus Christi. The Fourth Lateran Council affirmed the doctrine of transubstantiation in 1215 and inspired devotional practices that venerated the Eucharist as the actual body of Christ. In the late thirteenth century, Thomas Aquinas proposed the Feast of Corpus Christi to Pope Urban IV as a festive commemoration of the Last Supper. Removed from the solemnity of the Tenebrae, the period from Holy Thursday through Good Friday and Black Saturday, immediately before the Resurrection (Easter), it is celebrated two months after the Holy Thursday in late May or June during the long days approaching the summer solstice. The dating suggests possible connections with the later Midsommer Shows, the London pageants that were "provided by the guilds to which the Lord Mayor and sheriffs for the year belonged" (Chambers 1903: vol. 2, 165), and with St. John's Eve on June 23, which recalls the pre-Christian festivities, especially bonfires, associated even today with the summer solstice. David Wiles writes that it is "an appropriate day for celebrating the idea that the urban community was a single body, analogous to the body of Christ" (2001: 79). This is especially pertinent to the Noah pageants as the ark is often likened to the institution of the Church.

What is unique about the Feast of Corpus Christi is its celebration by a theatrical street procession in which a priest carries the Eucharist displayed in a monstrance out of the church under a protective canopy.[2] Still held in many Catholic parishes, Corpus Christi processions bring the Eucharist, which Catholics believe to be the actual body of Christ, out of the sacred space of the church and parade it through secular space. Unlike Palm Sunday, Corpus Christi is a joyous occasion, well removed from Lenten mortifications. Today, the Feast of Corpus Christi is often celebrated on a Sunday when the parish and perhaps the larger community may participate in a street procession. In contemporary Ireland, for instance, the procession is marked not only by ornate canopies, colorful vestments, and precious vessels, but also by a second display of the children's often-elaborate First Communion outfits. The Feast of Corpus Christi is not only a day when pageant producers might reasonably hope for good weather, but also the festive occasion when believers had access to divine immanence by experiencing the physical presence of Christ in their workaday world, in the here and now. It was ideal for the mystery cycle plays.

The cycles were typically performed every year, with exceptions for years of plague, civil unrest, or other emergencies. Considerable variations in the performance dates exist: "At Chester and Wakefield both procession and play originally took place on Corpus Christi day, the play later being transferred to Whitsun. At York, they remained together until 1426, when it was agreed to have the play on the vigil of the feast and the procession on Corpus Christ day" (Cawley 1983: 24). Each of the towns developed well-established routes through relatively narrow streets that the pageants would follow, stopping at designated stations, which were separated from one another by as few as a hundred meters. The sites where individual plays would be performed up to twelve times, often at churches or medieval gates, were already invested with importance. Various theories still debate the possibility of performing dozens of separate pageants at each of the twelve stations in York, where on June 5, the sun rises at 4:35 a.m. and sets at 9:30 p.m. Records show that hundreds of performers, stage hands, musicians, and other practitioners were obliged to be in place by 4:30 a.m., just before dawn. Several of the episodes would be performed at night, with the final pageant, the Last Judgment, coming sometime after midnight.

Street Theatre, Community Theatre

The term "pageant" could refer both to the biblical episode or to a wagon that served as a mobile stage. Great care and expense were lavished on these valuable properties that the guilds stored, improved, and reused year after year. The pageant wagons rode on two or more axles and are thought to have been as long as fifteen to twenty feet and about ten feet wide (see Figure 2). The principal playing area, the flat bed of the pageant wagon, typically had a column at each of its four corners that supported a roof, although probably not weight-bearing throughout. Nonetheless, the cycle plays performed on wagons ingeniously explored verticality by configuring playing spaces above, on, below, and perhaps adjacent to the wagon. In several of the pageants, God would appear on the upper-most level, above the wagon floor in a throne, his *locus*. Often elaborately decorated, colorfully painted, and well equipped, individual pageant wagons might have sophisticated machinery to raise and lower actors, such as the one playing God in the Doomsday pageant, from one performance level to another. Tydeman comments that the materials used for God's *locus* in heaven "were usually as expensive as could be procured or afforded; they were intended to give this area of the stage qualities of radiance and unearthly splendour"

Figure 2 *Pageant wagon (with ark already constructed) used in a modern-day performance of "Noah's Flood." Photo by Loop Images/Universal Images Group via Getty Images.*

(1978: 169). Chester begins with the prefatory stage directions: "*And firste in some high place—or in the clowdes, if it may bee—/ God speaketh unto Noe standinge without the arke with all his familye.*"[3]

In addition to the wagon bed and a celestial space above, the street level offered yet another playing area, one frequently associated with the devil and hell. The medieval cycle plays refer to this world as "middle earth," with heaven above and, in the case of Newcastle, the devil below the platform stage at street level or possibly emerging from beneath the wagon. Wiles asserts that in performing the Newcastle play, on the street level "Noah's wife and the Devil merge with the crowd of spectators. The crowd are not separated from the dramatic action, but are made to feel that they are the sinner whom the flood is destined to destroy" (2001: 79). In other plays, a hell mouth provided access to the area below the wagon's stage. Such vertical configurations could visually suggest the Great Chain of Being, with the God and the angels above, humans on the pageant wagon, and the devil below. Not all of the cycles were always performed on pageant wagons. There is consensus that the N-Town plays "were produced *c.* 1450–75 in a fixed location on multiple stages, in the manner of the French and German Passion plays" (Cawley 1983: 22). The logistical complications and limitations of performing on mobile stages would have made scaffold performances more attractive, particularly for the most spectacular of the cycle episodes. Even if pageant wagons were used, supplemental playing areas, such as Mrs. Noah's hill, may have been created apart from the pageant wagon.

Different circumstances of production of medieval drama generated a spectrum of theories of the physical relationship between the audience and the performance. In York, there are records of payment for positioning the pageant wagon at various stations to provide ideal, even seated spectatorship from the second floor of the buildings directly opposite or in bleachers that offered "stadium seating." Tydeman asserts that in York "sometimes pairs of citizens or even syndicates leased the stations, and charged the public for the privilege of occupying places, which enabled the lessee to make a profit, even after laying out money on refreshments and on building scaffolds to accommodate spectators" (1986: 111), which underscores an additional economic dimension to the production. Rosemary Woolf argues that the evidence of three painted cloths or curtains used at the back and on the sides of the stage indicates that the ideal viewing perspective, especially for tableaux, might have been less than 90 degrees: "wagons were roofed, and the roof must have rested on pillars at each corner. Such an arrangement must have given an effect of a picture-frame just as did the later proscenium arch" (1980: 100). Most scholars believe that in stational productions the wagons might have been crowded by spectators on three sides, affording unpaid public access even if the sightlines were not ideal. The performance was probably directed to an audience on the left side of the wagon, although this, too, is a point of debate.

If the celebration of the Mass or liturgical drama served as any predicate, then there was a clear differentiation between celebrant or performer and spectator that could be manipulated as well as observed in pageant production. Of course, the concept of a fourth wall was entirely unknown to medieval audiences, and there are numerous instances in which characters speak directly to the audience. In the Towneley Noah, with the flood waters rising and Noah and his wife in flagrante fisticuffs, Mrs. Noah seems to step outside the action, as if the other performers are in freeze-frame, to counsel the women in the audience directly:

I se on this sole
Of wives that ar here,
For the life that thay leyd,
Wold thare husbandes were dede,
For, as ever ete I brede,
So wold I oure sire were. (393–8)[4]

Momentarily suspending the physical combat with her husband for her to deliver this advice to the audience only heightens the absurdity of their quarrel and perhaps introduces an element of meta-theatricality. At other instances, performers emerged from the crowd, effacing the barriers between audience and actor. Likewise, many of the amateur performers might have been recognized by the audience. Rebecca Schneider points to one consequence of amateur performance:

Consider, for example, that an actor standing in a role in a medieval tableau might very well play that same part in everyday life. That is, the medieval actor cast to hammer the nails into Christ's hands might well have been an actual nailwright. So the tableau image of the biblical laborer would have been an image of the biblical laborer and the contemporary laborer simultaneously—and in this way, surrogacy was laminated atop simultaneous actuality. (2011: 146)

The least sophisticated spectators, children and adolescents, might be the first to call out to a neighbor performing as a biblical figure.

The cycles invited everyone, rich and poor, learned and unlearned, young and old, male and female, to see events from the Bible as their history, their heritage. Erich Auerbach observes that medieval Christian drama "opens its arms invitingly to receive the simple and untutored and to lead them from the concrete, the everyday, to the hidden and the true—precisely as did that great plastic art of the medieval churches" (1991: 155). Some scholars see the relation of individual pageants to the full cycle as comparable to that of a single panel in a high cross or a cathedral's façade to the entire work. Woolf, for instance, asserts that "the effect of actors dramatically grouped in a medieval wagon must have resembled that of a compartment in a series of frescoes" (1980: 100). Meg Twycross sees the "pageants as a picture sequence, the same in kind and intent as those of the Books of Hours or stained-glass windows which feature the events of Incarnation or Passion frame by frame: a parallel emphasized by the framing effect of the pageant wagon" (2008: 35). Medieval drama offered a spiritual and educative experience similar to that of the visual arts, especially painting, but its festive, communal dynamic intensified the audience's affective experience. The medieval cycles created a utopian celebration of shared beliefs, moments when discord could be subordinated to the consensus and celebration of the community itself. As much as devotional enthusiasm, the guilds and other cycle participants may have been motivated in pursuit of *communitas*, however momentarily, in the pageant audience.

Auerbach cites Abbot Suger's justification for the costly gilding of the doors of St. Denis that portrayed Christ's Passion and Ascension: "*Mens hebes ad verum per materialia surgit, / Et demersal prius hac visa luce resurgit*," translated by Erwin Panofsky as "the dull mind, through material things, rises to truth / And, in seeing this light, is resurrected from its former submission" (Panofsky 1946: 48–9). Suger's rationale not only informs the medieval Christian arts, but also offers a further explanation for the expense and energies expended on the production of the mystery cycles. Whereas a Book of Hours could stimulate the intellect and the aesthetic sensibility, pageants could avail of the wide spectrum of sensory overload potential in the theatrical form.

Just as devotional piety and civic pride figure in the popularity of the cycle plays, so do the pleasures of theatre. As well as being devotional and civic exercises, the cycle plays were also entertaining. Although the hundreds involved in giving the performances would work arduously throughout the day, many others would be enjoying a respite from work in a festive atmosphere. Martin Stevens advocates for a "Carnival approach" (1987: 82) to the York cycle as an instance of Mikhail Bakhtin's *carnivalesque*. The Noah pageants contain more humor than most others, and their elements of spectacle were likely to have delighted audiences in almost magical ways. The pageants were, after all, theatrical events that created powerful sensory experiences and illusions in ways that liturgical worship simply did not.

The Spectacles of Noah

One of the ten episodes common to all four of the major medieval English cycles—Chester, N-Town (also known as the *Ludus Coventriae* or the Hegge cycle), Towneley, and York—concerns Noah, as does a surviving fragment from Newcastle upon Tyne.[5] These are known by various titles in modern editions, but here are grouped as the Noah pageants. In York, Noah's story occupies two pageants, labeled by Beadle as "The Shipwrights: *The Building of the Ark*" and "The Fishers and Mariners: *The Flood*" (2009: vii). Perhaps there were two plays from an early date in the cycle's life or perhaps over time the pressures of performing within a limited time span on a single day may have split the Noah story into two pageants in

York. Alternatively, perhaps the York cycle may have created distinct, separate episodes to accommodate the very different, potentially farcical tone of the second of its Noah episodes.

The Noah pageants display an especially rich array of scenographic, thematic, and typological possibilities that demonstrate how the cycle pageants embraced the domestic and the universal, the secular and the sacred, the mundane and the apocalyptic. In some regards, the Noah pageants are representative of the cycle plays, but their access to the Old Testament, domestic humor, and potential for spectacle, while hardly unique, are not typical. The vast majority of cycle plays depicts events from the life of Christ; most, in fact, stage events from the Passion of Christ, episodes from Palm Sunday to Easter. The Noah story, moreover, belongs to a small group of cycle episodes, including Cain's killing of Abel and Abraham and Isaac, drawn from the Old Testament. Under the influence of the Church Fathers, the Old Testament's importance had been diminished to be valuable principally insofar as it prefigured the New Testament. Noah is one of the Old Testament patriarchs, although at times he seems more like a hen-pecked husband because of another way in which the Noah pageants are atypical: the incorporation of comedy. The Noah pageants run the comic gamut from the farcical Punch-and-Judy slapstick through wordplay and insults to the divine comedy of man's salvation. The popularity, survival, and robust afterlife of the Noah pageant may owe as much to its comic elements, including its "happy ending," as its potential for multiple stage spectacles. Many of the cycle episodes stage key moments in the Christian faith that are filled with unbelievable events that inspire awe, fear, and pity: the crucified Jesus comes back from the dead; a cataclysmic flood destroys all but eight humans; a father prepares to kill his beloved son. In the specific instance of the Noah pageants, the representation of human work infused with God's grace to realize salvation in the face of the apocalyptic flood demanded an aesthetic of the spectacular. The Noah pageants, in fact, may stage as many as three spectacular events; only a small

number of cycle episodes match the Noah pageants' potential
for the miraculous and apocalyptic, and demand such inventive
scenographic technologies.

The flood narrative appears not only in the Bible, but across
world mythologies and related apocalyptic literature. Outside
of the biblical account in Gen. 6:9–9:17, *The Epic of Gilgamesh*,
which was unknown in Europe until the nineteenth century,
and the account in the Islamic Quran are perhaps the best
known, but the film *Parasite* (Joon-Ho, 2019) demonstrates
the endurance of flood narratives. The Noah story produced
a very wide spectrum of visual representations in paintings,
carvings, and glassworks of a massive ship, a procession of
animals, and the flood. There are marked variations in these,
just as there are in the action, characters, and tone of the
iterations of the Noah story in the mystery cycles.

The main action in the medieval Noah pageants is what
appears in the Bible: the building of the ark, the entry of the
animals in the ark, the flood itself, the dispatch of birds (first
the raven and then the dove), and finally the exit from the ark
and return to land. Genesis is replete in its specificity, especially
in matters quantifiable: the age of Noah and his father; the
exact dimensions of the ark; the familiar forty days and forty
nights. None of these can be realistically represented on stage.
Nor can the actions that hold the potential for spectacle: the
building of the ark, the procession of the animals, and the
destruction of the flood.

All iterations of the pageant begin in the disorder brought
about by human sinfulness and God's subsequent wrath.
Following the episodes of the expulsion from Eden in Chester
and York, and of Cain and Abel in N-Town and Towneley,
the Noah episode is located in a distinctly postlapsarian
world where Noah is isolated from fellowship with the rest of
humanity because of his faith and virtue. Like all of the Old
Testament episodes in the cycle plays, the Noah plays see the
extended family as the primary societal unit. Especially in the
Chester Noah, the family also comes to resemble a medieval
guild as a cooperative entity working together.

Among these iterations, there is a very wide range of characterizations of God and of Noah's relationship to God. In N-Town, God's angel delivers the commission, but in all other versions, there is direct contact and varying degrees of intimacy between God and Noah. An anthropomorphized God expresses his displeasure with human's sinfulness in all of these iterations; only in Newcastle does God not speak directly with Noah. In Chester, God sees his creation "sett fowle in sinne" (4); in Towneley, "full low ligges he [man], / In erth himself to stuf / with sin that displease me" (85–7). In N-Town, Noah's wife and sons join him in praying to God who sends an angel to commission Noah to build the ark. In N-Town and Towneley, however, Noah's prayers alone bring forth God's response. In Towneley, petulant God speaks directly to the audience, rather than in dialogue with Noah, to express regret that He ever created Man:

> Venjance will I take,
> In erth for sin sake,
> My grame thus will I wake,   *anger*
> Both of grete and small. (88–91)

Here a demanding God speaks almost like a spurned lover:

> Every man to my bidding
> shuld, be bowand   *bowing*
> Full fervent;
> That made man sich a creatoure,
> Fairest of favoure,
> Man must luf me paramoure,   *love me devotedly*
> By reson, and repent. (77–82)

In Towneley, God appears directly to Noah, speaking "*from above*" (73), in his locus and then "*God descends and comes to Noah*" (118); when God speaks directly to Noah, He calls Noah his "freend" (117). Similarly, in Chester, God speaks directly to Noah from the play's opening lines, calling him "my servante free, / That righteous man" (17–18). In York, the relationship between Noah and God is the most fully developed. They seem like old friends in conversation. Noah candidly protests his age, infirmity, and ignorance, but just as freely accepts God's grace: "He wille be my beylde, thus am I bowde [bold]" (119).

As punishment for human sinfulness, God intends a flood that will obliterate all life except for his chosen: Noah, his extended family, and the pairs of animals. Unlike God's charge to Adam and Eve, which is a prohibition—not to eat from the Tree of Knowledge—God asks Noah to undertake a task that seems impossible. In Towneley and York, Noah protests that he is unqualified for shipbuilding. He is old, feeble, and inexperienced. The grace of God, however, enables the weary, unknowledgeable Noah to build the ark and, thanks to the ingenuity of the shipwrights, to do so in only minutes of stage time.

Noah undertakes the challenges to build the ark, to load the animals and his family, and to weather the flood. All three of these actions offer inviting opportunities for spectacle that could captivate the audience through their imaginative execution. The transformation of the pageant wagon or stage into the ark might well have been a *coup de théâtre*. The ark-building is very closely narrated in all four cycles. God tells Noah, as He does in the Bible, the exact dimensions of the ark: 300 cubits long, 50 cubits broad, and 30 cubits high. Although in N-Town, Noah and his family exit to construct the ark off stage and return to the stage to assemble it, most scholars agree that in other versions, the pageant wagon itself was transformed into the ark in a short space of time. Perhaps using prefabricated, possibly hinged or cantilevered sections, a clinker-built ship was constructed before the audience's eyes. Davidson (1996) and Unger (1992) document the tools, implements, and materials then at the disposal of the York shipwrights; both suggest that whenever possible the guilds would proudly display the technologies and tools of their trade as props in creating the ark on stage. Noah's transformation of the stage into an ark is miraculous; audiences would have viewed its construction in only minutes of stage time as nothing less. In Towneley, the scenography is further complicated because, after construction of the ark, there must also be a hill on which Mrs. Noah stubbornly perches with her distaff, the emblem of her gender, spinning her yarn as the flood waters rise. She enters the ark at the last moment. Here, and in the other conflicts between Noah and his wife, the utter absurdity of their quarrels at such a pivotal moment for all humankind undergirds the pageant's comic dimension.

Residents of York may well have been familiar with the painted-glass panel in the Great East window of the York Minster that depicts four anxious human figures, two men and two women, on a single-mast, square-rigged vessel looking down at a drowned man. The bearded Noah stands at the ark's stern, his eyes uplifted to God and his hands clasped in prayer. At the ark's bow a hound, the only animal represented, stands on forepaws with its head looking back to Noah. The effect of the painted glass panel is a miniaturization of the ark. Moreover, the place of that single panel in the vast magnificence of the Great East window may be likened to that of a single pageant within the entire cycle.

The second potentially spectacular action is the loading of the animals into the ark. Again, in most variants, the pageants follow the detailed biblical prescription in God's command to Noah. The stage directions in Chester indicate a procession, possibly accompanied by music, as the sons and their wives load the ark:

> *the arke muste bee borded rounde aboute.*
> *And one the bordes all the beastes and fowles*
> *hereafter reahersed muste bee paynted,*
> *that them words may agree with the pictures.*[6]

This suggests a procession of "animals" painted on boards carried onto the ark by Noah, his sons, and their wives. Lisa J. Kiser, however, argues that Chester contains a more fully developed catalogue of animals, and some of its pageants "used live animals" (2011: 30), which surely might create another kind of spectacle. In addition to the procession of animals, the raven and the dove Noah releases might be live birds or props "flying" on a thin wire. Contemporary stagings of the Noah story, widely adapted for juvenile audiences and especially popular in primary schools, often use the parade of the animals into the ark as the centerpiece. The 2016 York Minster Mystery Plays featured an inspired array of animals, some crafted in hessian, cane, and papier-mâché. The sixty-six animals included crocodiles, elephants, rhinoceroses, flamingos, giraffes, birds, and chickens. The whales required as many as six people to "perform" a single animal.[7]

How the flood might have been realized on stage has attracted less critical attention than have the construction of the ark or the animals' procession, but it, too, might have been sensationally staged. Muir describes the inventive staging of the flood in a Noah pageant produced in Mons, France: "the stage is covered with turf and in one section where the wicked are feasting it is carpeted with violets. At the signal of the director, the water pours down through lead pipes, concealed by clouds, from barrels located in Heaven. The wicked disappear through trapdoors in the stage as if drowned" (1995: 211). Alternatively, long cloths, perhaps translucent, of blue might have been stretched and undulated in front of the ark to simulate the rising water. Sound effects could also evoke thunder, lightning, and even rising water. Cynthia Tyson argues that not only the Noah episode, but four of the Towneley pageants "present intriguing references to water as a staging property" and that, rather than cloth, "a much greater likelihood exists that real water was present in the acting area to serve as a staging property" (1974: 101). The ark and its inhabitants might have swayed as if buffeted by the sea and the storm. As challenging as the staging of the flood was, it seems unlikely that medieval producers could overlook its opportunity for spectacle.

The ark, animals, and flood all figure in the Bible, but the most celebrated comic intervention in the medieval cycle plays is the recalcitrance of Noah's wife. To Allardyce Nicoll, the incorporation of comedy was as indispensable to the cycles as was spectacle: "the great cycles of the fourteenth and fifteenth centuries could not have become the popular things they were had it not been for the efforts of the comic actors to make sport and of the machinists to make wondrous entertaining shows" (1963: 179–80). Of the York pageant, Beadle points to the

> attractive blend of humour and wonder, humour in the way in which God's staggering and peremptory command bewilders the massively aged and unsuspecting patriarch, wonder in the way in which the obedience of the old man generates a sudden access of grace, transforming him into a skilled craftsman whose one hundred years of work on the ark are completed in the passage of twenty lines of verse. (1985: 52)

Although many commentators as well as Noah himself note his weariness, old age, and physical decline, Noah is not always meek with his wife. Mrs. Noah, observed V. A. Kolve, is "the root-form of the shrewish wife, and her relationship with Noah became the archetype of marital infelicity" (1980: 146). The misery that is their marriage, Kolve argues, presents a microcosm of the disorder in the postlapsarian world. Noah's relationship with his wife is presented as the continuation of long-standing marital strife, which, in Towneley and York, spills over into what looks like routine domestic violence. As troubled as contemporary readers are by the play's assertion that wives owe their husbands obedience, the ensuing domestic violence, especially in Chester and Towneley, is potentially even more disturbing. Some see the conflict between Noah and his wife as central to the humor as it occurs at the very moment crucial not only to Mrs. Noah's salvation, but to her (and the audience's) very survival. Towneley builds considerable suspense as Mrs. Noah's refusal to enter the ark is strung out over ninety-six (327–423) of the play's 555 lines.

Towneley also has the most combative of the encounters between Noah and his wife, which culminates with Mrs. Noah sitting on her husband. Both before the ark-building and after its completion, their domestic strife moves from name-calling to slapstick. Mrs. Noah initially complains that Noah is a poor provider who does whatever he wants: "Yit of mete and of drink / Have we veray skant" (197–8). After Mrs. Noah recommends to the wives in the audience a tit-for-tat programmatic harassment of their husbands: "What with game with gile, / I shall smite and smile, / And quite him his mede [*pay him back*]" (214–16), Noah is quick to call her "ram-skyte [*ram-shit*]" and to strike her. The context clearly indicates that this is not the first time that Noah has raised a hand to her; she shows no surprise and is quick to strike back with the threat, "Thou shal three for two" (226). Mrs. Noah goes off to her work, spinning, and Noah goes to his work, building the ark.

In Chester, as in Towneley, the division of labor between men and women is emphasized. In Chester, where Noah's entire family participates in building the ark, the men take on the work that requires tools (an axe, hatchet, and hammer) while the women build a fire, secure a kitchen chopping block,[8] or carry timber because, as Noah's wife says, "women bynne weake to underfoe / any great travell" (67–8). As several scholars note, human labor, "wyrke," is vital in this postlapsarian world and especially important in this particular play. Sarah Beckwith writes that "the meaning of the word for 'work,' then, is densely encoded to mean at once humanity as the object of God's work, the work of making humanity, the work of restoring it, and Noah's work of ark building and salvation" (2001: 44). Man must build the vessel of his survival on earth; the need is even more pressing in an Old Testament world since Christ has not yet redeemed mankind. And there is a further sense of work: that of the pageant-makers, whose work takes on meta-theatricality.

As soon as the ark is ready, Noah needs to board his family, but in Towneley, despite the rain, Mrs. Noah resists, saying that she has work to do. After the pleas of her daughters-in-law do not move Mrs. Noah to enter the ark, Noah and his wife go at it again. She wishes that Noah were dead and ends up sitting on his back but "bet so blo / That I may not thrive" (412–13). Only when their three sons discover them locked in violence, perhaps displacing the biblical episode of Noah's shame when his sons discover him drunk and naked, do the sons shame the parents in to entering the ark. All of the animals, humans included, enter two by two.

Whereas commentators like Chambers once found Mrs. Noah "hilarious," feminist critics in recent decades have not. Jane Tolmie, for instance, points out that Mrs. Noah alone has bonds outside the family, specifically in the Chester pageant, through her sisterhood with the Good Gossips. Her girlfriends drink malmsey and sing with her, suggesting both that women's work is undervalued (as does Towneley) and that Mrs. Noah alone expresses compassion for the humanity lost in God's vengeful flood. As Tolmie observes, Mrs. Noah's lament for the loss of her friends, "brings out some of the irresolvable tensions between human and divine mandates" (2002: 15).

In *Gender in Medieval Drama*, Katie Normington (2009) argues that there is little documentation to suggest that women performed as actors in the English mystery cycles and much more evidence to indicate that men played the female roles. Women unquestionably were involved in the production of the pageants in stage management, the lending or making of costumes, and so on, but decorum proscribed their appearance on stage. Performance of Mrs. Noah by a man surely must condition her characterization on stage and the domestic violence in her marriage. We do not and cannot know how her character was performed. What, Meg Twycross (2018: 225) asks, if Mrs. Noah were played in the style of a pantomime dame? Alternatively, she may have been portrayed as an attractive, much younger woman saddled with a 600-year-old husband. Perhaps she was a bruising harridan. Her scenes in Towneley and York suggest a sharp comic departure from Noah's piety. In contrast to Noah's obedience and reverence toward God, in Towneley and York,

Mrs. Noah refuses to accept her husband's authority over her. Together, Noah and his wife make each other's life a misery; their marriage is the font of their unhappiness and, except in N-Town, the pageant's central *agon*.

The N-Town Mrs. Noah shows no animosity to her husband and accepts his role as the head of the family. All four of the wives in N-Town, in fact, speak obediently to echo and amplify what their husbands say. This so alters the gender dynamic in the N-Town Noah that Christina M. Fitzgerald can argue that Noah's wife is a type of Mary, the mother of Christ. Moreover, while the ark is constructed off stage, the subplot in N-Town is another major departure from the other versions as Noah's father, the blind Lamech, kills Cain and a young guide. The strongest link between plot and anomalous subplot in N-Town are the many references to God's vengeance. Some form of the word "vengyd" appears no fewer than ten times in a play of only 253 lines. Noah and his family fear that "God wyl be vengyd on us in sum way" (21) and, indeed, God says "I wol be vengyd of þis great mysse!" (95). Lameth expresses a similar fear in almost exactly the same words: "Alas, what xal I do, wrecch wykkyd on woolde / God wyl be vengyd ful sadly on me" (190–1).

The Noah fragment from Newcastle moves in yet another, very different direction. Immediately after God's angel commissions Noah, the Devil persuades Mrs. Noah to drug her husband by telling her that Noah's plans will mean the deaths of all the family. This clearly recalls the Devil's temptation of Eve. She, in fact, believes that Noah's newly acquired ark-building skills are the work of the Devil. The Devil speaks directly to the audience, as he often does in the cycles and likely would have worn a mask; the array of devil masks documented by Nicoll and others would leave the audience in no doubt of the devil's identity. Alfred David asserts that, in the Newcastle fragment, the Devil is "a buffoon like the vice-characters in the morality plays" (104). The fragment breaks off just as Noah goes to usher his family into the ark.

In the other versions, at the play's conclusion, as the flood waters subside, a raven and then a dove are sent out in search of land. Unique to the Chester Noah pageant is the rainbow that God sends as a symbol of the bond with Noah's descendants: "by verey tokeninge that you may see / that such vengeance shall cease" (311–12). The rainbow, too, would have been inventively realized, perhaps in cloth or, as in the 1433 Doomsday pageant, as a "rainbow of tymber" (Johnston and Dorrell 1971: 31). God's renewed love for man is symbolized in the olive branch the dove brings back to the ark or the rainbow he sends. In Towneley, Noah identifies the land as the "hillys of Armonye" (466), often read as a pun with "harmony" (Robinson 1991: 35). Once on land, Noah and his family offer song or sacrifice in thanksgiving for their survival. The new order at the play's end is a comic one. It is a better order because the threats to it, including the unhappiness of Noah's marriage, have been, at least for the moment, quelled. Yet before them lies a world of work. Noah surveys a scene of utter devastation:

nowther cart ne plogh
Is left, as I ween,
nowther tree then bogh,
Ne other thing,
Bot all is away. (535–9)

His family's survival and, with it, their audience's, is assured, but demanding wyrke lies before them.

The texts disclose several instances that call for song, music, or dance as are commonly found in pageants. In Chester, the Good Gossips drink malmsey and sing as they part from Mrs. Noah. Noah may sing from Psalm 79. Likewise, in N-Town, a song of mirth and joy is the final note: "For joye of þis tokyn ryght hertyly we tende / Oure Lord God to worchep: a songe lete vs synge" (252–3). John Russell Brown (1983: 26) suggests that in Towneley a parade of the seven deadly sins, a regular feature of the morality plays, might accompany Noah's opening description of man's sinfulness.

The typology of the individual pageants invites the audience to locate the Noah episode in relation to other episodes in the cycle. Noah's faith anticipates that of Abraham, whose episode immediately follows. Like other Old Testament figures, Noah is tested by his response to God's commands. The wood Noah used to build the ark, and specifically in the case of Chester, the mast, prefigures Christ's cross. Likewise, the ark-building echoes Creation; in N-Town, Noah styles himself as "The Secunde Fadyr" (17), suggesting his links to both Adam and God. Unger (1992: 35) notes that Noah's popularity with Church Fathers like Jerome and Augustine assured his place in medieval thought: "Augustine called the ark 'a figure of the city of God … that is to say, of the Church'" (33–4); Jerome elaborated this comparison to liken the animals in the ark to the diverse constituents within the Church. The widest variations in the typology concern Noah's wife. In the Newcastle fragment, the conscious malice of Noah's wife surpasses Eve's and may have even had, like the Devil, a comic dimension. Here the conflict between Noah and his wife replays, perhaps comically, in the strife between God and the Devil. Within the mystery cycles themselves, later pageants refer back to this one. Kolve points out that in the York cycle, *Judgment Day* contains "a long speech by God again gets the action under way, and this speech deliberately echoes ideas and phrases from the earlier *Flood* Episode" (1980: 68). In the New Testament accounts of Matthew and Luke, Christ likewise compares Noah's Flood and the Last Judgment.

A complete cycle, performed in a single day or over two or three days, recapitulates the entire history of the known world from Creation through the fall, Christ's life and death and even anticipates the end of the world. As a theatrical genre, pageants often stage the passage of centuries or even millennia, but few others take on all of human time. While looking both back to the past and forward to the future, several pageants plainly evoke the here and now, late medieval times in England, to show the relevance and immediacy of the events depicted to the lives of the audience. In medieval England, as in the twentieth and twentieth-first centuries, the episodic structure of pageants evokes a sense of timelessness, blurring, or effacing chronology. A variety of techniques to manipulate time as well as space can be found in the mystery cycles.

A dominant convention at work in the medieval cycles is the engagement of the audience in another-worldly sense of time in which both the past is brought to life and the future realized in the present. Often, as in the Noah episodes, there is a vast gulf between the time span announced in dialogue and performed on stage. Several of the Noah plays stipulate his exact age. In Newcastle, for example, Noah reminds God that he is "six hundred winters of eld" (78). Perhaps this helps to initiate the audience to the entirely different sense of time at work in the Noah pageants. In an analogous situation, the engagement with books of hours, Kathryn Ann Smith asserts that "medieval people conceived time in terms of the span of Christian salvation history. ... medieval devotional and religious manuscripts could contract or expand this sacred time, elide or create connections between different historical periods or sacred events, or emphasize particular incidents or individuals" (2003: 57). Perhaps a forty-year-old neighbor performs as the 600-year-old. In both Chester and York, Noah says that a hundred winters pass while he builds the ship, over perhaps five minutes of stage time. Other episodes, especially those comprising the Passion, are graphically staged; the action approaches realism; stage time is much closer to real time. In the Noah episodes, however, the audience would have embraced the oft-experienced compression of time as part of the pageant's presentation of the miraculous.

Pageants often manipulate time; many deploy a familiar rhetorical strategy to realize a stylized treatment of time: anachronism. In York, both Noah and Mrs. Noah, for example, vow by St. John, who had not yet been born. Anachronism is clearly a conscious choice, intrinsic to a sophisticated rhetorical strategy to show the immediacy of distant events to the lives of medieval spectators. In *Mimesis*, Auerbach writes that "what these violations of chronology afford is in fact an extremely simplified overall view adapted to the simplest comprehension" (1953: 158). James J. Paxson argues that anachronism "functions self-consciously and metadramatically like Shakespearian anachronism ... as a poetic device or trope in the mystery plays [that] discloses a complex *structural* state of affairs, a state that in turn advertises anachronism as a poetic property uniquely situated in a native dramatic tradition" (1995: 321). Perhaps the most remarkable anachronism in the Noah pageants is that the Old Testament God who speaks to Noah so often and so plainly displays the mercy, forgiveness, and love of the New Testament God.

The treatment of space in the medieval cycle plays is similarly unfettered to the literal. For example, at the end of the Towneley *Second Shepherds' Play* both time and space are dissolved as the three fifteenth-century shepherds from the British Midlands become the three magi. They move across the millennia and thousands of miles to attend the birth of Christ. The potential for entertaining and delighting the audience, in fact, lies largely in the disparity between what the audience is told is happening and what it sees, and faith and imagination are what bridge that gap. It is not a ship 400 meters long, but it is a representation of that. The audience's delight lies in the human ingenuity and imagination that can realize such a representation in such a short space of time. The mystery cycles project an image of communal celebration of salvation, prosperity, and human ingenuity. However momentarily, audience and performers are united in utopian *communitas*.

The cycle pageants cease to be performed when suppressed by the Protestant Tudors as part of the Reformation and its attempt to purge Catholic teachings (see Gardiner 1967; Duffy 2006), especially their visual expression. Representations of the deity are commonplace in Catholic churches and more generally in Western art, but aniconism, the prohibition of physical representations of God, other supernatural beings, and even saints, appears in Buddhism, Hinduism, Islam,

Judaism, and other major faiths. Having a deity represented graphically or personated by an actor, even today, would be considered blasphemous by many major faiths. Even at the beginning of the twentieth century in England, so rigid were Lord Chamberlain's strictures against representations of the deity on stage that Laurence Houseman's nativity play *Bethlehem* was banned in 1902. Jonas Barish described this as "the anti-theatrical prejudice" (1981); Clifford Davidson observed a more sweeping "anti-visual prejudice." He points to "an unparalleled iconoclastic fervor that wished for the destruction of all images with sacred content" (1989: 33), including those produced by the mystery cycles. The York cycle was last performed in 1569. The Chester plays were performed as late as 1568 and again in 1575. In several instances, local authorities petitioned, at great risk, to continue to perform their pageants, but by 1600, "two centuries of religious drama, and a whole chapter in lay appropriation of traditional religious teaching and devotion, were at an end" (Duffy 2006: 582).

Whereas religious subjects dominated pageants produced in England until the Reformation, by the fifteenth and sixteenth centuries in Italy and elsewhere pageants had become lavish secular spectacles for which artists like Leonardo da Vinci might find a remunerative place at court. Walter Isaacson describes a 1490 pageant for Ludovico Sforza on which Leonardo worked:

> The curtain rose on a celestial curved vault that Leonardo had constructed in the shape of a half egg that was gilded with gold on the inside. Torches served as the stars, and in the background the signs of the Zodiac were illuminated. Actors portrayed the seven known planets, turning and revolving in the proper orbits ... It culminated with the gods—led by Jupiter and Apollo and followed by the Graces and Virtues—descending from their pedestals to shower verses of praise on the new duchess. (2018: 114)

Like the royal progresses and court entertainments that later flourished in Tudor and Stuart England, the Sforza and Medici pageants were secular spectacles that recruited the finest actors, artists, and musicians to serve the court audience. Unlike the professional productions for a private, very elite audience, the earlier English mystery pageants were religious street theatre: painstakingly prepared, but nonetheless amateur productions accessible to an entire community. After the suppression of religious drama in England, the pageants and pageantry of the cycles supplied prototypes that morphed into the Midsommer Show, the Lord Mayor's parades, royal progresses and processions, the great civic spectacles chronicled by Bergeson, Hill, and others. Although religious figures and tropes routinely appear in late-sixteenth- and seventeenth-century drama, the fundamental focus of the civic drama shifted profoundly. In England, the urgency with which the pageant cycles were suppressed testifies to their power and popularity.

Afterlife

The cycle plays have had a very vibrant afterlife in the twentieth and twenty-first centuries. In June 1951, E. Martin Browne directed a revival of the York mystery plays in the ruins of St. Mary's Abbey in York as part of the Festival of Britain, which was held in commemoration of the Great Exhibition of 1851 and in celebration of the postwar recovery. When Canon J. S. Purvis published a modern-language adaptation of the cycle in 1957, he recalled in the Foreword that "this version was offered with grave misgivings as to its possible success; the first performance showed how unnecessary those misgivings had been. The performance was hailed by critics as a quite startling revelation of the power and beauty of the medieval Plays" (1957: 7). The revivals of the mystery cycles in York, as well as elsewhere, notably Coventry, Leeds, Chester, and Toronto, have become regular features supported by the religious groups, civic officials, the community, and the tourism industry. The modern-day revivals capture some of the enthusiasm that the plays generated in the long ago and has been well-documented by Browne, Margaret Rogerson, Twycross, Jane Oakshott, Johnston, and many others. Their analysis of the pageants' revival brought new attention to the circumstances of medieval productions and has shaped much of the scholarship over the past fifty years. For instance, in 1975, the York cycle was performed in Leeds by community and university volunteers by recuperating the processional staging on pageant wagons. Oakshott reports that

> the use of a different cast for each episode has a Brechtian effect, in which the action portrayed is more important than the personalities of those performing ... because the audience is addressed directly and at close quarters, its members become part of the cast, and integral to the action. They are the crowd cheering at the entry to Jerusalem, for instance, and they witness—and condone—the Crucifixion first hand. (2013: 369–70)

The distanciation that comes from having several actors perform the same character, does indeed suggest Brecht's *Verfremdungseffekt*, as does the audience's recognition of its own complicity in the death of Christ.

The Noah episode has been especially attractive in modern revivals. Some of the adaptations have been very loose: a production in Chester in 2012 envisioned Noah's Flood as a "30 minute musical," performed by three principals (God, Noah, and Mrs. Noah), forty-three sinners, thirty-six others as well as twenty-nine primary school children performing as animals.[9] The revivals of the pageants in York and Chester are now regular events remarkable for the level of community engagement generated.

The Chester Noah play inspired two modern musical adaptations. Benjamin Britten's *Noye's Fludde* (1958), described by Heather Wiebe as an "experiment in arts education" and "an exercise in community" (2006: 77), was a performance piece that could involve a large number of children. Wiebe cites the response of Kenneth Clarke, who found *Noye's Fludde* "an overwhelming experience"; Clark wrote, "it was not only a work *for* children; it also used children to rekindle a remembered childhood for an audience of adults" (qtd. in Wiebe 2006: 92). The Chester Noah also served as the basis for Igor Stravinsky's *The Flood* (1962), which was broadcast on national television in the United States by CBS in a performance choreographed by George Balanchine.

Contemporary playwrights have likewise found inspiration in the medieval cycle plays. Tony Harrison's *The Mysteries* (1977) drew on the Towneley cycle in a very successful production at the National Theatre in 1977 that later transferred to the Lyceum and was broadcast by Channel 4 in 1985. Terrence McNally's *Corpus Christi* (1998) is a retelling of Christ's life as a gay man set in contemporary America, specifically Corpus Christi, Texas. The Chester Noah and Britten's *Noye's Fludde* have another afterlife in Wes Anderson's film *Moonrise Kingdom* (2012).

2

Counter-Hegemonic Pageantry: *A Pageant of Great Women*

In the late nineteenth and early twentieth century, leisure and, with it, theatre-going changed. Theatre building boomed. From twenty theatres in London in 1851, "by 1901 there were forty-two music halls and thirteen theatres under the Lord Chamberlain, and a further twenty-nine theatres in the suburbs" (Woodfield 1984: 4). American vaudeville and British music hall and variety theatre flourished not only in major cities, but in provincial outposts. The late nineteenth century also saw profound changes in the audience's experience in the theatre, for instance, when the auditorium was now dimmed. Moreover, the late nineteenth and early twentieth century polarized the audiences of pageants and mainstream theatre.

Pageants were related to other thriving popular entertainments—ranging from touring productions of West End or Broadway hits to Mrs. Jarley's Waxworks—but they were especially closely related to tableaux vivants. A series of tableaux vivants, "living pictures," might construct a symbolic narrative that constituted an entire dramatic presentation of silent, elaborately costumed performers arranged in painterly configurations. A single tableau or "picture" might be struck at the end of a scene in a conventional stage play. Several tableaux might appear on a bill with musical performances, lectures, and dancing. Often tableaux vivants were performed as fundraisers in which nonprofessional, sometimes entirely untrained, performers appeared on stage, typically as mythological, allegorical, or historical figures, to benefit a prominently named charity. Because a large number of ordinary people—amateur actors, seamstresses and tailors, carpenters and set dressers, and so on—could contribute to these symbolic configurations, tableaux vivants were popular across wide spectra of class and political affiliation. Whether commercial advertisement, command performance, or music hall entertainment, played by professionals or amateurs, tableaux proliferated in the 1890s in the English-speaking world. They were accessible and entertaining, potentially powerful, and often cheap.

At the beginning of the twentieth century, the meaning of "pageant" had broadened to include any bombastic public display. The popular press routinely referred to both the coronation (1902) and the funeral (1910) of Edward VII as a pageant. What would overtake the generic sense of "pageant" was the local historical pageant, which is often dated to 1905 when Parker's pageant at Sherborne enlisted the services of hundreds of local volunteers. Like the tableaux vivants, these pageants allowed amateurs—young or old, new voters or those seeking the vote, men or women, rich or poor—not only to see their past brought to life, but to be part of it. Parker famously said that "nobody is too good to be in a Pageant and almost everybody is good enough" (1928: 284). In historical pageants, both spectator and performer displayed their aspirations and civic engagement through public performance. Unlike conventional plays of the day, local pageants were expressly written to include a large, often indeterminate, number of amateur performers as supernumeraries. As in the medieval cycles, enthusiastic amateur participants seized the prestige that came with helping to create a spectacle. Moreover, supportive friends and family of the amateur performers swelled the audience well beyond those who would attend commercial theatre performances.

Whether Parker drew on E. K. Chambers's *The Medieval Stage*, published only two years before his Sherborne pageant, remains uncertain, but in *Several of My Lives*, Parker recalls Richard Wagner's influence as formative: "now [*c*.1875] Wagner, gave me a new insight into the possibilities of music; and Wagner entirely revolutionized my conception of musical drama. Yes, and of spoken drama, and of all that has to do with the stage. I will go father: he revolutionized my life" (1928: 90). When he visited Bayreuth in 1884, Parker experienced Wagner's *Gesamtkunstwerk*, the total work of art, not bound to a single discipline but drawing on many: orchestral music, vocal performance, architecture, set design, costuming, acting. For Wagner, true art fulfilled the atavistic needs of the *volk* and on a very grand scale. In Bayreuth, Parker saw it all done outside the cosmopolitan center. If in Bayreuth, why not in Sherborne? Bayreuth inspired a model that Parker reworked twenty years later.

The year after his success with *The Sherborne Pageant*, Parker "invented and arranged" his second pageant, *The Warwick Pageant*. And invent and arrange he did. The description of the pageant as a "celebration of the thousandth anniversary of the conquest of Mercia by Queen Ethelfleda" might raise a historian's suspicions, but appending a commemorative anniversary, especially a centennial or millennial, was a further rationale for local pageants. In his "Introduction" to *The Warwick Pageant*, Parker asserted a familiar claim to authenticity when he averred that he had "clung as closely as the exigencies of time and space would allow to history and tradition" (1906: 10). First up was the all-male narrative chorus of Druids who introduced a short vignette of the death of Kymbeline, "First King of Britain" in AD 40 (13). His son, Caradoc, becomes king, thwarts the Druids' attempt to sacrifice a young child, is taken prisoner by the Romans, escapes and returns to convert his people to Christianity. And that's just the first episode. Episode 2, set in AD 500, sees the Britons defeat the Picts and Scots and consolidate powers of both Church and State. In the third episode Ethelfleda, who "moves among

her people, everywhere greeted with adoration" (19), founds
the Warwick School. In AD 920, Guy of Warwick slays the
monstrous Dun Cow and wins the loyalty of the people and
the hand of Phyllis. Parker freely rewrites and borrows from
Shakespeare and Marlowe in episodes depicting Roger de
Newburgh, Edward II, Richard Neville, and Lady Jane Grey.
For Episode 10, Parker's acknowledged source in presenting
Robert Dudley is John Fisher's "The Black Book of Warwick."
The final episode depicts the 1694 fire of Warwick. William III
bestows his largesse and exhorts the people:

> Now, Mr. Mayor, to work! Summon the people!
> Let the world see how Warwick's sons and daughters
> Rise from disaster, from despair pluck hope!
> From Warwick's ashes build the newer Warwick!
> Begin! Begin! Sound trumpets and begin! (57)

The chorus of Druids announces that their work is done. A
grand procession, the culmination of this continuous past,
brings all the performers, thousands of people, to the stage:
Britannia and her escort of colonies, the girls of the high school,
a large dramatic chorus, and then all the pageant performers
who together sing several songs concluding with the national
anthem.

In *The Warwick Pageant*, 2,000 performers played to
audiences estimated at 44,000 in six performances outdoors
on the site-specific Warwick Castle grounds. Like all of
Parker's town pageants, it made extensive use of music, here
traditional songs, original music by Parker, the 100th Psalm,
and "God Save the King," many performed by the 2nd
Battalion of the Warwickshire Regiment. Dialogue, which was
not mechanically amplified, was extensive in Parker's Warwick
pageant. Withington wrote that

> the "historical exposition" is the soul of the Parkerian
> pageant; and, this being the case, the dialogue is important.
> Some there are, in America, who maintain that a pageant

should be wordless, because in many cases it is impossible for the audience to hear; the Englishman [Parker] feels that speech is so important that the audience should be restricted to those who can get within earshot. (1920: 218)

This is plainly at odds with an average attendance at *The Warwick Pageant* that surpassed 7,000. Only those in the most expensive seats would be privileged to hear the spoken dialogue.

More important was the sustained, sweeping engagement of the community in producing the pageant:

the population of Warwick was busily preparing for a whole year. Two thousand citizens gave their services without remuneration of any kind; most of them even providing for the expense of their own costumes. ... for a week the entire town, without distinction of class, sex, or age, lived as in a dream through a species of Elizabethan phantasmagoria, reviving the deeds, the costumes, and the figures of a distant and glorious Past. (Borsa 1908: 192)

Only months after his success at Sherborne, Parker, then fifty-three and not yet a British citizen, saw a place in theatre history within his reach, and he seized it. Before the Society of Arts in London, he claimed "the invention of what to all intents and purposes is a new form of drama" (1905: 145). Not only was it new; it would rescue the people from what Yeats would call "this filthy modern tide" (1956: 323). By December 1905, Parker had already generated highly prescriptive rules to govern his (and all) pageants. He specified "a narrative chorus of men's voices only" to provide crucial exposition. He stipulated performance at a site of historical consequence and meaning. All props, costumes, and accoutrements were to be sourced and manufactured locally. His new form of drama dispensed with professional actors, scenery of any description, and the representation of incidents from recent centuries. Pageants ended, he declared, with the communal singing of the national anthem (Parker 1905: 145).

Parker did not invent a new form of drama. Like the pageantry he had seen performed in Bayreuth and by Edward VII, Parker's historical pageants recuperated features from multiple genres. He reached back to Greek drama to appropriate the chorus. He capitalized on antiquarian interests to imagine "authentic" clothing and accoutrements. His musical knowledge channeled community voices and instrumental performance. He borrowed popular music, song, and dialogue shamelessly. Eclectically, Parker drew on the ritual activities associated with both local and national celebrations. Withington saw Parker's historical pageant as "a chronicle-play, differing from the Elizabethan chronicle-play only in the fact that the hero is a town, not an individual" (1920: 299). But whatever the exact nature of his intervention in theatre history, Parker did invent a money-spinning career for himself as pageant-master. After Sherborne, Parker received invitations to produce pageants from seventy-three towns (Yoshino 2003: 50). Over the next nine years, Parker performed a total of six town or village pageants; dozens of others sprung like mushrooms. Much in demand as a pageant-master who served the civic needs of the Edwardian era, Parker charged £1,744 2s. 6d. (or about £209,000 in 2020 currency) in fees and expenses for his services for the *York Pageant* (1909), more than double the pageant's declared profit and many times what was actually donated to charities.

Parker's pageant movement first took root, not in the burgeoning metropolitan centers, but in English towns and cities like York, Warwick, or Dover. Parker and his fellow pageant masters, among them Frank Lascelles and F. R. Benson in Britain, would prove in great demand to produce historical pageants. Frank Lascelles, for instance, created immense pageants in the UK as well as Canada and South Africa. The United States followed with equally ambitious pageants such as Thomas Wood Stevens's and Percy MacKaye's *The Pageant of St. Louis, A Civic Masque* (1914), "a production of unprecedented proportions" (Glassberg 1990: 173) performed by 7,000 and seen by 500,000. Having already published his own *A Manual of Pageantry* in 1914, Withington would observe that in Europe and North America "pageants swept the land ... people went pageant-mad" (1939: 510).

The intense popularity of historical pageants between 1905 and 1914 nearly coincides with a similarly expansive growth of the women's suffrage movement in the UK. The two are hardly unrelated. Both movements engaged the performative impulses of the Edwardian *volk* and reflect an underlying optimism and civic engagement. Both relied on the mobilization of large numbers of supporters—not merely the powerful, rich, enfranchised, and hegemonic, but also elements of that population that did not even have the vote, including women and children. Both partook of and advanced an increasingly visually oriented culture. There was also a reciprocity at work between the pageant craze and the women's suffrage campaign. Both historical pageants and the women's suffrage movement created events that were made newsworthy only through the concerted enthusiasm of massive numbers of people. Both were abruptly suspended when Britain's entry into the First World War demanded the public's loyalty. There was, of course, one critical difference: the historical pageants were hegemonic; the women's suffrage movement was counter-hegemonic.

The proliferation of inexpensive newspapers and their ability to reproduce photographs and illustrations were as essential to the popularity of pageants in the early twentieth century as they were to the women's suffrage movement. The demand for Parker's services owed much to the worldwide distribution of photographs from his earliest pageants. Indeed, there was profit to be had in the material culture produced by these pageants: postcards, "books of the words," souvenirs, lavishly illustrated programs, even photographic prints. A comparable range of suffrage items was available from stalls at the suffrage exhibitions, from suffrage shops, and by mail order as advertised in the suffrage press. In regards to women's suffrage, Katherine Kelly argues that "The London-based suffrage movement of 1906–14 reveals a collaboration between the cause and the British press 'at the height of its power and prestige'. Together, they provided the national stage with a new kind of gendered spectacle designed to fuel and satisfy the metropolitan desire for novel esthetic display on a mass scale" (2004: 329–30).

The campaign for women's suffrage in the UK organized in the nineteenth century and intensified after expansions of the male franchise in 1867 and 1884. In 1894, women in the UK won the right to vote in borough and county elections. The National Union of Women's Suffrage Societies (NUWSS) was founded in 1897 to seek full enfranchisement for women throughout the UK. Emmeline Pankhurst's militant WSPU followed in 1903. Pankhurst's autocratic leadership, her insistence on ladylike white dresses and feminine deportment, but, most importantly, the drift of her organization toward physical violence, drove some suffragists to break off from WSPU to form the Women's Freedom League (WFL) in the fall of 1907. Not only was the WFL committed to nonviolent, constitutional methods, but also to a wider feminist agenda that went well beyond securing the vote: women's health, equality in the workplace, and the taxation of women without representation.

Lisa Tickner traces the mass mobilization of women in the cause of suffrage in the UK to Christabel Pankhurst's 1907 correspondence with former Conservative prime minister Arthur Balfour. Balfour wrote to her: "if it can be shown either that women as a class seriously desire the franchise, or that serious legislative injustices are being done them ... the change should be made" (qtd. in Tickner 1989: 79). Over the next seven years, voteless women would vote with their physical bodies in processions, parades, and pageants. The first of these mass suffrage demonstrations, the NUWSS's Mud March, so-called in consequence of inclement weather, attracted 3,000 participants to London on February 9, 1907. The Artists' Suffrage League (ASL, founded in 1907) supplied some eighty banners that became a visual focus in the 1907 Mud March. In June 1908, an astonishing 30,000 gathered in Hyde Park for the Women's Sunday rally. The next year, shortly after the first tableaux presentation of *A Pageant of*

Great Women for the WFL Green, White and Gold Fair at Caxton Hall, the Pageant of Women's Trades and Professions, held on April 27, 1909, again displayed the ASL banners, supplemented by newly created ones. The American suffragist Rheta Childe Dorr described some of the new banners: "The ancient emblem of those engaged in fishery trades—the two crossed fishes surmounted by crowns—will be carried by the Scotch fishwives in their characteristic dress. Those learned in the culinary arts have decided upon a golden gridiron which they will display on long staves; tailoresses, a pair of scissors" (1909: 178). Physicians donned their scarlet academic robes; pit-brow women wore their shawls; artists carried their palettes. In the Pageant of Women's Trades and Professions women performed as themselves. Press accounts invariably reflect the visual diversity among these groups, cleverly costumed in their uniforms, academic regalia, ordinary work clothes, to remind spectators and the wider public how diverse and essential women's work was in Edwardian Britain.

Tickner provides abundant evidence, first, that mass processions and spectacles showed the politicians and the public that women did indeed want the vote. Second, Tickner graphically demonstrates that the suffrage movement quickly developed its own distinctive visual vernacular. The suffragist movement in England appears to have been much more visually oriented than that in Ireland or the United States. In England, suffragist organizations developed distinctive, rival color schemes. In the program to the WPSU's Women's Exhibition in 1909, Mrs. Pethick Lawrence wrote that "The Woman's Movement has developed a ritual and a symbolism of its own ... women have brought into the political arena, which they have now consciously entered, a new element of dignified ritual and aesthetic beauty."[1] The iconography of suffrage banners, jewelry, and clothing offered rich photo opportunities and projected its own burgeoning traditions (Figure 3). Over these years, the ASL banners would marshal and celebrate an increasingly inclusive spectrum of working women (charwomen and barmaids as well as artists and

Figure 3 *Mary Lowndes's banner celebrating one of Hamilton's famous women, Marie Curie, 1908. Photo by Museum of London/ Heritage Images/Getty Images.*

physicians), university alumnae, regional contingents, and great women from history and myth. Tickner argues that the suffragist banners and needlework celebrated a "women's history" in their iconography, their inscription and their collective workmanship; they focused a sense of shared identity and imbued it with political significance. ... [the banners] acted as a gloss on the procession itself, developing its meanings, identifying and grouping its participants and clarifying its themes ... the banners emphasised the broad base of suffrage support, the diversity of women's achievements and the benefits the women's vote would bring to society at large.

(1989: 60)

At least two of these qualities that Tickner attributes to the needlework—the creation of a "women's history" and the celebration of the diversity of women's accomplishments—would be key to *A Pageant of Great Women*.

Cicely Mary Hamilton

Cicely Mary Hamilton (1872–1952), nee Hammill, was a working woman who supported herself first, briefly, as a teacher, and then as an actor and professional writer. For ten years, she toured England and Ireland with fit-up companies playing in provincial towns. Her experience of audiences, theatre production, and entertainment while on her theatrical tours was formative. She may not have attended university, but she certainly knew what worked on stage. In *Life Errant* she recalls that she usually "played the 'heavy'" (1935: 38) and was "badly paid" (42) for her efforts. The low wages, poor working conditions, and an array of dangers more threatening to women than men shaped Hamilton's views on working women, whether actor, landlady, or housewife. Hamilton was always more interested in the realities of the working woman than the allure of the "New Woman."

Hamilton was one of the youngest and one of the few unmarried women featured in a front-page pictorial in *Illustrated London News*, "Woman Militant: Leaders of the Suffragist Procession and Their Symbolic Banners Commemorating Great Women of All Ages," on June 20, 1908.[2] By then, Hamilton was a featured speaker at suffragist gatherings sponsored by the WFL. Like many an actor, she was an effective orator. Despite her relentless modesty, she admits in *Life Errant* that she "was popular as a suffrage speaker" (69), but soon realized the sameness in a monotonous string of speeches from suffrage platform. In 1908, Hamilton and Bessie Hatton founded the Women's Writers Suffrage League (WWSL), not only to encourage suffragists to write articles for the suffrage newspapers, but to create short plays, interludes, and other dramatic entertainments that could enliven their meetings. On December 23, 1909, *The Vote* recalled the formation of the WWSL:

> One night Miss Hatton was at the Dramatic Debates where she heard Miss Cicely Hamilton speak on the suffrage. She was immensely struck by her earnestness and the power she exercised over the small audience, which was composed largely of "indifferents". The next day she wrote to Miss Hamilton and said how much she enjoyed her speech. She received a prompt reply to which was expressed the desire to found a Women Writers' Suffrage League, "if only someone would undertake the secretaryship." This wish was immediately fulfilled by Miss Hatton. (Hill 1909: 100)

The short plays, poems, satires, and even operettas produced by members of the WWSL infused greater variety and entertainment into innumerable suffragist gatherings.

Hamilton also belonged to the Actresses' Franchise League (AFL), which was founded in 1907.[3] Like the WWSL, the AFL set out to be "strictly neutral in regard to Suffrage Tactics" and "to assist all other [suffrage] Leagues whenever possible."[4] Similarly, the constitution of the WWSL, "drawn up by Miss Hamilton early in 1909," states "Its methods are the methods proper to writers—the use of the pen" (qtd. in Robins 1913: 106). In her "Foreword" to the 1948 edition of *A Pageant of*

Great Women, Hamilton writes that "there were two respects in which the Woman Suffrage Movement differed from the general run of political strife. It was not a class movement; every rank and grade took part in it. And it was the first political agitation to organize the arts in its aid" (1935: 31).

Although she founded and was prominent in various organizations, Hamilton withdrew or ceased to be active in several of these. In 1990, Harriet Blodgett, one of the first to devote scholarly energies to her, aptly described Hamilton as an "independent feminist" (1990: 99). Hamilton abhorred groupthink, what she referred to as the "crowd-mind" or "crowd-life, [with its] overpowering sense of membership. ... [when individuals] resigned their responsible individuality" (1935: 73). She joined the WSPU, but did not last long: "For a few months I was a member of the Women's Social and Political Union; then, for somewhat longer, of the Women's Freedom League; but I was happier working with less political bodies, such as the Women Writers' Suffrage League, of which I was one of the founders" (66). She came to see the WSPU's Emmeline Pankhurst as "a magnificent demagogue" who used the organization as her own cult:

Not the Fascists but the militants of the WSPU first used the word "Leader" as a reverential title; and the *Furhrerprinzip*, the principal of leadership, was carried to something like idolatry by the wearers of the purple, white, and green. Emmeline Pankhurst, in this respect, and on a smaller scale, was forerunner of Lenin, Hitler, Mussolini—the Leader whose fiat must not be questioned, the Leader who could do no wrong! (127)

Although she rejected Pankhurst's dicta, especially those concerning feminine dress and deportment, Hamilton's engagement was undeterred. She sought a more democratic, participatory, inclusive activism. She found it in print by publishing in newspapers such as *The Common* Cause, *The Englishwoman*, *The Vote*, *Votes for Women* (even if it was the official newspaper of the WSPU until 1912), and later *Time and Tide*, on stage as a suffragist speaker, as the author and performer of original suffragist plays, entertainments, and *A Pageant of Great Women*. Notwithstanding her contempt for Emmeline Pankhurst, Hamilton performed at WSPU events, wrote for WSPU publications, and agreed to productions of *A Pageant of Great Women* under WSPU sponsorship.

As a writer, Hamilton was remarkably adept at recognizing and adapting popular forms and genres to suit her purposes, the first and most pressing of which was, in 1906, to support herself and her sister, Evelyn Hammill. Her early career as a writer produced what she could sell, what she herself describes as "hack writing":

> My literary, like my previous theatrical, ambitions had to reconcile themselves with the need for earning a living and a living for more than myself; hence, for some years, the greater part of my output took the form of contributions to cheap periodicals, many of them catering for the tastes of the young. Sensation was their keynote: stories of bandits, pirates, savages and detectives, preferably youthful detectives. (1935: 57)

One of the things that makes a writer a hack is the ability to identify and to conform to an established formula—that is, to subdue the writer's own creative impulses and to gratify the audience's expectations. Seán Moran documents that between April 1906 and December 1907 Hamilton wrote ten stories for the *Union Jack*, a boys' paper, "famous for its 'resident' detective Sexton Blake" (2017: 71).[5] She continued to write for and about children all of her life.

In February 1908, Lena Ashwell produced Hamilton's first full-length play, *Diana of Dobson's*, at the 573-seat Kingsway Theatre, where it received very good notices. Its run of 143 performances ended only because Ashwell took a break before leading one of four touring companies that brought the play to the provinces where, Hamilton writes, it "ran for years" (1948: 62). Hamilton sold the rights to both the play and its novelization outright. In London, Century Publishing brought out Hamilton's novelization of *Diana of Dobson's* in 1908; Grosset and Dunlap in New York followed later that year. The New York edition, copyrighted not by Hamilton but by Century Publishing, misspelled the author's name as "Cecily Hamilton."

By then, Hamilton was living on Glebe Place in Chelsea, about 300 meters from the Old Ranelagh Gardens where the episodes of the *Chelsea Historical Pageant* played at ten venues from June 25 to July 1, 1908. The Chelsea pageant was a typical hegemonic pageant from the 1905–14 era, but one staged without the exorbitant fees of a pageant-master like Parker or Lascelles. Performed multiple times in the borough that it celebrated, it announced a philanthropic mission with profits going to the Royal Chelsea Hospital. As a charitable venture, it published what it could sell: a program, colored postcards, and an elaborate book of words (replete with notes by the ten authors of its ten episodes, forewords, music, and even "a foreword to the forewords"). Its program contains pages and pages listing committee members, sponsors, and supporters, many of them titled. Some women and children, but principally men performed ten episodes that spanned the millennia by imagining moments in Chelsea's past: a meeting between Caesar and the Druids, a May Day dance, Thomas More's Farewell to Chelsea. Hamilton may or may not have attended the Chelsea pageant, but she was probably aware of the crowds in her neighborhood that did attend and, as a working writer, the growing popularity of historical pageants as a theatrical genre. In collaboration with Edith Craig, Hamilton created a pageant that celebrated the history not of a place, but of a gender. As a counter-hegemonic pageant, it subverted the conservatism of the idiom.

Show-Woman and Woman

The women's suffrage movement in England was driven by meetings at which suffragists deployed not just highbrow literary or visual forms, but also lowbrow amusements: cartoons, peep shows, fortune telling, skits, rhymes, and zines. Hamilton's writing crossed generic boundaries freely and often, especially in pursuit of the comic. In this she was not alone, but she certainly was among the first. Lis Whitelaw notes that "much of Cicely's suffrage journalism at this time [1907–9] was written to amuse and entertain her readers" (1990: 103). Susan Carlson coined the term "comic militancy" to describe the spirit of dozens of short suffragist plays, noting that "the vast majority of the plays appearing in suffrage papers were comic, and many drew power and appeal from their use of popular literary formats" (2000: 210). In November 1907, Hamilton published a satirical column, "How the Vote Was Won," in *Women's Franchise*. Here, as elsewhere, Hamilton's rhetorical stance is rooted not in moral outrage, but in cool logic and barbed irony. Her prose piece "How the Vote Was Won" ridiculed the ludicrous anti-suffrage contention that British women are all supported by men by taking it to its *reductio ad absurdum*. Framed as "some short extracts from Prof. Dryasdust's 'Political History of the Twentieth Century', published in the year 2007 A.D." (1907: 227), it begins as Dryasdust recalls that in the early years of the twentieth century "it was the men of the country who now began to agitate for Women's Suffrage—since only at that price could they free themselves from the burden of maintaining some millions of women in idleness" (228). In 1908, Hamilton reworked this material with illustrations by C. Hedley Charlton in a pamphlet, which might also be described as a comic book, zine, or even graphic novel, published by the WWSL under the same title. The next year, in collaboration with Christopher St. John (Christabel Marshall), Hamilton adapted *How the Vote Was Won* as a one-act stage play whose premiere was directed by Edith Craig at the Royalty Theatre on April 13, 1909. For Katherine E. Kelly, "using elements typical of the suffrage conversion trope, this one act nevertheless outshines others with its broad comic sweep (all are mocked, including suffragists) and its brilliant comic dialogue" (2007: 679).

In Hamilton's words, it became "the [Actresses' Franchise] League's first smash hit ... steeped in the nineteenth-century tradition of farce" (1935: 66).

Like the multiple versions of *How the Vote Was Won*, *A Pageant of Great Women* exists in different iterations; both works show Hamilton as collaborator. Edith Craig, the daughter of Ellen Terry, directed many of Hamilton's plays and is credited as "arranger" (or "director") of the premiere of *A Pageant of Great Women* and all of its subsequent authorized performances. In a few instances, she is listed as co-author. After a dozen years in the United States where she acted under the name Ailsa Craig, she returned to London in 1907 at the age of thirty-eight to operate a costume rental shop in Covent Garden. Craig directed and costumed commercial theatre productions as well as tableaux entertainments in the West End. From about 1907, Christopher St. John was Craig's partner. Both collaborated with Hamilton on several occasions; all three women were born between 1869 and 1872.

In 1908, Hamilton created her first suffrage stage show, *Miss Hamilton's Anti-Suffrage Waxworks*. Like tableaux vivants, waxworks were a popular fundraising entertainment in the UK and North America, ones expressly designed to be modified to suit the needs of even small groups without professional actors in modest, often appropriated, performance spaces. W. G. Benham introduced a compendium of waxworks by writing, "there is scarcely any form of amateur entertainment so successful, so simple and so generally suited to the requirements of amateur performers, as the representation of *Mrs. Jarley's Waxworks*" (1873: 2). Moran (2017) provides the most cogent description of the *Anti-Suffrage Waxworks* in which the Show-Woman (or Show-Man), an articulate compere, presided over speechless stock characters, such as The Ideal Woman, Queen Elizabeth, The Suffragette, The Policeman. Played by actors, the stock characters initially appeared as lifeless waxworks that were animated only after the Show-Woman wound them up. Once brought to life, each of the waxworks moved only with jerky, mechanized motions in a short vignette that fulfilled the stereotypical expectations familiar from the popular press. What is especially noteworthy is that Hamilton created not a pro- but an anti-suffrage persona. The Show-Woman affected to oppose suffrage and adopted a mocking, condescending attitude toward the suffrage movement, a rhetorical posture not unlike Stephen Colbert's on *The Colbert Report* (2005–14). Records suggest that The Suffragette was designed "to look a perfect wreck, wearing a huge chain around her waist, the hook of which the showman explains can be used to hitch on to railings or carry away portions of the House of Commons" (qtd. in Moran 2017: 92) (Figure 4). Hamilton's *Anti-Suffrage Waxworks* proved very popular and continued to be staged through 1911. Like many of Hamilton's works, the *Anti-Suffrage Waxworks* used humor to deliver a clear but clever propagandistic message. And like *How the Vote Was Won*, the *Anti-Suffrage Waxworks* relied on the ruthless logic of farce to depict characters sequestered in one-dimensionality. The waxwork figures invited audiences to seize agency by laughing at how crudely the popular press caricatured suffragists.

The *Anti-Suffrage Waxworks* and the pageant that Hamilton created the next year had many features in common. Both could be performed with only a few skilled actors. Because they made minimal scenographic demands, the *Anti-Suffrage Waxworks* and the pageant could readily be staged in different venues. They provided a theatrical respite from the highly charged, but all-too-familiar exhortations typical of suffragist gatherings. More importantly, they were accessible, whatever the theatre-going experience of the audience and, thus, cut across the class lines that were a source of concern for the English suffrage movement and have obsessed many recent critics. Most important, they gave audiences positive agency in the power of laughter. Rather than dwelling on women as victims or the need for suffragists to project a feminine image to the public, the *Anti-Suffrage Waxworks* exposed what the audience knew: how unfairly they were maligned in the press and popular imagination.

Hamilton herself often performed the Show-Woman. The archives have yet to disclose a script; in fact, there may never

Figure 4 *Illustration of a performance of* A Pageant of Great Women *and the* Anti-Suffrage Waxworks *at the Albert Hall in Sheffield.* Yorkshire Telegraph and Star, *October 17, 1910. The suffragist squaring off against a policeman (from the* Anti-Suffragist Waxworks*) wears a hook that could be attached to railings at protests.*

have been a fixed text, only Hamilton's extemporaneous narrative. There certainly is evidence to suggest that, like the pageant, local and topical references could be interpolated in different performances. Perhaps the decade Hamilton spent touring the provinces playing "the heavy" gave her the Show-Woman's voice and helped to shape her performances.

"'Tis Good to Be Alive When Morning Dawns!": *A Pageant of Great Women*

The year 1909 was an *annus mirabilis* for Cicely Hamilton. In January 1909, the *Illustrated London News* noted her continuing success with *Diana of Dobson's*, which was revived by Lena Ashwell for thirty-two performances at the upscale Savoy Theatre and simultaneously on tour across Australia. That same month, she attended the first of the AFT's "At Homes" at the Criterion restaurant. Hamilton was "on the founding editorial board of the suffragist periodical *Englishwoman*" (Thomas 1995: 134), which published her short play "Mrs Vance" on February 1, 1909. With Christopher St. John, Hamilton wrote *The Pot and the Kettle*. Her other collaboration with St. John, *How the Vote Was Won*, was making the rounds at suffragist meetings as "beyond doubt one of the greatest successes of the AFL's repertoire" (Moran 2017: 95). In April, Hamilton performed as the Show-Woman in the *Anti-Suffrage Waxworks* at the WFL Old World Fair where a tableaux version of *A Pageant of Great Women*, its first iteration, was organized by Edith Craig. In May, Hamilton set aside her animus toward the Pankhursts to perform the *Anti-Suffrage Waxworks* at the WSPU exhibition at the Prince's Skating Rink. Later that year, Hamilton collaborated with Charlton, Mary Lowndes, and Dora Meeson Coates to produce another zine, *Beware! A Warning to Suffragists*.[6] In May 1909, Hamilton's 257-page treatise *Marriage As a Trade*, described by John Simkin as Hamilton's "most important contribution to the feminist movement" (2020: n.p.) was published by Chapman & Hall in London. In August, *Marriage As a Trade* was among the books of the month featured in the *Review of Reviews*. The American edition published by Moffat, Yard in New York, attracted immense press coverage throughout the United States. The *St. Louis Post Dispatch*, for instance, described it as "conceived in cold blood and written in cold ink."[7] In September, Hamilton was instrumental when the WFL published its first issue of *The Vote*. In October, she participated in the founding of another organization, the Women's Tax Resistance League (Whitelaw 1990: 104). Then in November, *A Pageant of Great Women* had its premiere.

On the afternoon of November 12, 1909, a Friday, a four-hour, star-studded theatrical bill played at the Scala Theatre, with a seating capacity of 1,139. On the program were three one-act plays: *The Pot and the Kettle* by Cicely Hamilton and Christopher St. John; *The Master* by Gertrude Mouillot; *The Outcast* by Beatrice Harraden and Bessie Hatton, all building to the premiere of *A Pageant of Great Women*. The resources of the AFL helped Hamilton and Craig bring on stage more than fifty performers including Adeline Bourne (who played Woman), Pauline Chase (then starring in the West End as Peter Pan), Marion and Ellen Terry and Eve Balfour as well as Hamilton's collaborators, Christopher St. John and Edith Craig, and Hamilton's sister, Evelyn Hammill, all elaborately costumed as great women. Like most pageants, the number of speaking roles was limited, but, unusually for a pageant, Hamilton's play was crafted for performances in multiple venues and, even more unusually, in purpose-built English theatres.

In retrospect, there is almost an inevitability to the creation of a suffrage pageant by Hamilton. There may have been immediate precedents for a woman's suffrage pageant. In 1892, J. Grant Henderson created *The Temple of Fame: A Pageant of Famous Women* for performance in Ontario, Canada.[8] There were also at least two Scottish suffrage pageants at the end of the century's first decade. Helen MacLachan's *Women Down through the Ages* or *A Pageant of Women through the Ages* was performed outdoors on the steps of the Edinburgh Hospital for the Deaf and Blind, now Donaldson's School,

possibly as early as 1908.[9] Before a large banner emblazoned
with the words, "The eternal feminine leads us ever on," fifty
performers, including young girls, costumed in period dress
personated mythological and historical women of the near and
distant past. MacLachan, secretary to the Edinburgh Women's
Freedom League, later wrote the suffragist play "The Mad
Hatter's Tea Party up to Date" that appeared in *The Vote* on
April 12, 1912 (Carlson 2000: 210). Leah Leneman describes
another Scottish suffrage pageant staged in Edinburgh on
October 9, 1909 as "the pageant of Scottish women who
played a part in the country's history (even if only a mythical
one)" (1995: 80–1).

An obvious source for *A Pageant of Great Women* was the
banners celebrating great women created by the ASL for the
NUWSS demonstration on June 13, 1908. Caroline Herschel,
Jane Austen, St. Catherine of Siena, Katharine Bar-Lass (Kate
Barlass), Joan of Arc, Marie Curie, Angus of Dunbar, Florence
Nightingale, and Elizabeth Fry were all known through
stunning banners created by Mary Lowndes and Barbara Forbes
before appearing in *A Pageant of Great Women*. In a letter
to the *Times* published on June 15, 1908, two days after the
mass procession, NUWSS president Millicent Garrett Fawcett
defended the banners celebrating these women from the past:

> May I be permitted to point out that suffragists believe that
> the names of "distinguished women who did noble work
> in their sphere" are in themselves an argument against
> relegating a whole sex to a lower political status than
> felons and idiots? This is quite independent of whether the
> particular distinguished women named on the banners were
> suffragists or not. The names of Joan of Arc and Queen
> Elizabeth are found on the banners. The inference is surely
> clear. Lady Gordon affirms that her distinguished great-aunt
> Caroline Herschel was no suffragist. No one in their senses
> would expect a German lady born in 1750 to be one. Her
> services to astronomy were well recognized in the scientific
> world of her time. (Fawcett 1908)

Both Hamilton and Craig participated in suffrage marches before the pageant premiere. In June 1910, Hamilton (1910b) wrote in *The Vote* of her personal experience in carrying the banner of the WWSL.

The most frequently cited genesis of *A Pageant of Great Women* is described by Hamilton in *Life Errant*, where she recalls Craig's suggestion: "Edy came to me one day full of the idea of a pageant of great women which she would stage and which, she suggested, I should write for her. 'Suggested' perhaps is the wrong word to use: if I remember aright her suggestion was more like an order" (1935: 41). Hamilton never overstates her role as author and dedicates the published book of the pageant "to Edith Craig, whose ideas these lines were written to illustrate" (1910a: 9). Hamilton always acknowledged the collaborative nature of the pageant. Indeed, the programs and publicity materials for the 1909 tableaux performances at Caxton Hall, at Sheffield's Albert Hall, and in Middlesbrough attribute the productions to "Cicely Hamilton and Edith Craig." Likewise, the AFL annual report for 1909–10 refers to it as "Miss Craig's *Pageant of Famous Women*."[10] In 1909 and 1910, before its publication as *A Pageant of Great Women*, it was frequently known and performed as *A Pageant of Famous Women*. In the *Vote*, on November 18, 1909, it was simply the *Woman's Pageant*.[11] On at least two occasions (in April 1909 and April 1910), it was *Tableaux of Famous Women*.[12] These variations and slippages in titles affirm the collaborative nature of this work, the popularity of the genre, and the many ways in which pageants drew on or incorporated tableaux vivants.

Yet another inspiration was W. H. Margetson, whom Hamilton thanked in the 1910 Suffrage Shop publication of *A Pageant of Great Women*. In 1909, Margetson presented the cartoon, actually an oil painting, to the WWSL, the organization founded by Hamilton and Margetson's sister-in-law, Bessie Hatton. The painting provides the opening scenario and principal characters: Justice appears as a woman, blindfolded and holding the scales and a sword. Before her kneels Woman, looking back at Prejudice, a man, who restrains Woman by a rope of cloth (Figure 5). Hamilton acknowledged that his "Suffrage Cartoon suggested the employment of the figures of Justice, Womanhood and Prejudice" (1910a: 11).

The confluences of these sources for *A Pageant of Great Women* indicates how potent the vernacular visual culture of the women's suffrage was by 1909. Lowndes's design and needlework for the banners, Craig's costumes, and Margetson's painting were all critical inspirations for Hamilton's pageant. The pageant's success owes much to what never appears on the page: costume design and music. Twenty-two of Craig's costumes are seen in the photographs that appear in the 1910 edition of the pageant. J. M. Capel arranged the music for the premiere, but the only indication of the music performed in the program is for the legally mandated "God Save the King" at the matinee's conclusion.

The pageant is structured as a courtroom drama, with Woman pleading for her freedom. This provides a structural nexus of a court case with Prejudice arguing in favor of the status quo and Woman refuting his case, a familiar theatrical strategy successfully employed by plays including *Everyman* (1510) to *Our Town* (1938). Prejudice articulates the familiar anti-suffrage arguments. In support of Woman, six groups—the Learned Women, The Artists, the Saintly Women, The Heroic Women, The Rulers, and The Warriors—are "marshalled into cohorts, responding to each of the most common anti-suffrage arguments" (Cockin 1998: 96). These women are drawn from the near and distant past as well as the present; from England, France, the Netherlands, Spain, and India; from history as well as myth.

Woman explicitly seeks the freedom from Prejudice that only Justice can deliver. This is entirely consonant with Hamilton's interest in equality for women rather than in simple enfranchisement. That the word "vote" does not appear in the pageant, nor does "suffrage," "victim," or any form of "franchise," strongly reflects Hamilton's authorship. One of the reasons that the pageant was so effective and could be revived is that it imagines a liberation of women that goes well beyond enfranchisement.

Women Writers' Suffrage League.

Figure 5 *A WWSL postcard reproduction of W. H. Margetson's illustration of Justice, Woman, and Prejudice. Photo by W. H. Margetson/Buyenlarge/Getty Images.*

Justice instructs Prejudice to make his case: "Let him speak
on—let him accuse—then answer" (Hamilton 1910a: 23).
With Woman standing as the defendant, Prejudice argues that
freedom springs from wisdom and Woman has "scorned learning
… shunned knowledge" (25). Woman answers that Prejudice
"held [the woman's] body as all, the spirit as naught … [he]
saw us only as a sex" (25). Prejudice mocks women's learning.
Woman then introduces the Learned Women "who knew that
life was more than love / And fought their way to achievement
and to fame!" (28). In roughly chronological order, poets,
writers, scientists from Hypatia (370–415) through Madame
de Stael, Jane Austen, George Sand, to Madame Curie (1867–
1935) and "the girl graduate of a modern day" (29) appear on
stage in period costume. Woman then announces the artists,
poets, vocalists, dancers, and performers, from Sappho to
Nance Oldfield, and demands that Prejudice "think you well /
What you have done to make it hard for her / To dream, to
write, to paint, to build, to learn" (28). But Prejudice still
judges her unworthy because women are selfish creatures of the
domestic sphere: "cramped round and centered in her man, her
child, / Is room for no wide love of the outer world" (33).
Woman answers with the Saintly Women and the Heroines,
"those who have loved a cause, been loyal to it" (35), but
Prejudice still is not satisfied: "Her brain will reel beneath the
sense of power … she cannot rule" (37). Womanhood then
brings forth the Rulers, beginning with Elizabeth and Victoria
(the latter, "the little maid of eighteen years / Who, on a summer
morning, woke to find / Herself a queen" [37]) and finally the
Warrior Women. Several critics address the inclusion of the
Warriors as the largest group of women (which is accurate for
many but not all productions). They are the last and the least
expected of the six groups and respond to Prejudice's trump
card, his final argument for denying Woman equality:

> Force is the last and ultimate judge: 'tis man
> Who laps his body in mail, who takes the sword—
> The sword that must decide! Woman shrinks from it,
> Fears the white glint of it and cowers away. (39)

Woman responds in one of Hamilton's most defiant, forceful lines of iambic pentameter, "O bid him turn and bid him eat his words" (39), to introduce the first of the Warriors, Joan of Arc, costumed in chainmail. At the premiere, Hamilton placed herself in the warrior group as Christian Davies, costumed in tam o' shanter, frockcoat, and puttees. Undone by Woman's arguments, Prejudice "slinks away" (43), and Justice awards Woman freedom saying: "That soul alone is free / Who sees around it never a soul enslaved" (45). Woman relishes her freedom and twice (although Prejudice has left the stage) says "I have no quarrel with you [men]" (47). She ends on a note of exaltation by saying, "'Tis good to be alive when morning dawns!" (49).

The AFL's cooperation for the premiere meant that the majority of the great women were played by very well-known stage actors. The pageant, however, was designed to accommodate the amateurs who usually performed the great women. For the second performance at the Albert Hall in London in December 1909, the cast was memorably expanded beyond professional performers when Boadicea was performed by Teresa Billington-Greig, the first suffragist imprisoned in Holloway jail. After the London performances in November and December 1909, Justice, Prejudice, and Woman are the only characters who speak in *A Pageant of Great Women* and the only ones typically performed by professionals. In subsequent performances of *A Pageant of Great Women*, Hamilton often took the role of Woman (or Womanhood), the only substantial speaking role, accounting for almost 95 percent of the pageant's lines. Prejudice has 37 lines; Justice only 15, about 120 words. After the first two performances in 1909 with Ellen Terry as Nance Oldfield, who had eight lines, none of the great or famous women spoke at all. Woman, in fact, narrated the pageant not unlike Parker's narrators. Like many pageants, *A Pageant of Great Women* was a presentational piece of theatre spoken by a narrator, one not unlike the Waxwork's Show-Woman. And like many pageant narrator, Woman was unfettered in moving through time and space.

In presenting the great women, Hamilton's pageant, like so many, dissolves time and space. Hamilton had no regard for Parker's prescriptions about pageants, especially his insistence on the chorus of male voices and his decree that pageants not approach the present day. Not only was Marie Curie very much alive in 1909, but the girl graduates projected a future of even greater accomplishment for women. With little opportunity for detailed exposition, character development, or complex plots, pageants typically presume the audience's familiarity with the events depicted and the characters personated. In the instance of *A Pageant of Great Women*, the programs are especially relevant since they offered "Biographical Notes" that summarized the great women's accomplishments. Some of the women come from the mists of history, but with the exception of the biblical Deborah, the program notes associate specific dates and deeds with each of them. Hamilton gave bodily form to figures who may have been only vaguely known to the audience, just as the medieval mystery cycles did. This act of personation is key to pageants, especially the historical pageants that were in vogue in 1909. These great women are Egyptian, French, British, German, Swiss, Italian, Greek, Dutch; most are not British. There were thirty-nine women in the premiere, but in later productions, this number would grow to ninety. Rebecca Cameron argues that "Women's final words also suggest that the utopian performance of transnational, transhistorical sisterhood presented in Hamilton's *Pageant of Great Women* addresses the future more than it does the past, using history to present a fantasy of what women could be" (2009: 149). Hamilton's ending clearly did have utopian and fantastic dimensions, but any comparison with Parker's *Pageant of Warwick* reveals how firmly rooted in contemporary realities it was.

When Hamilton later negotiated a possible production outside of England, she wrote that the selection of the great women was made "with a spectacular effect in mind" (qtd. in Cockin 1998: 102). Together the women form a compendium of women's history that dwells not on wives and mothers, but on women who distinguished themselves in the face of all of Prejudice's beliefs. Cameron sees this as the basis of comparison between *A Pageant of Great Women* and Caryl Churchill's *Top Girls* (1982), but another especially rich comparison is with Judy Chicago's *The Dinner Party*, her installation now at the Brooklyn Museum. *A Pageant of Great Women*, like Chicago's *chef d'oeuvre* (begun in the 1970s), is a presentational piece whose meaning is generated largely by the striking, spectacular visual vernacular associated with great women across many ages, nations, and professions. Chicago created a massive triangular banquet table with a customized tablecloth, goblet, plate, and flatware for each of the thirty-nine women. The only use of language in *The Dinner Party* is the women's names, including five of Hamilton's great women (Sappho, Hypatia, Boadicea, Caroline Herschel, Elizabeth I), crafted in exquisite needlework. Like Hamilton's pageant, *The Dinner Party* moves freely through time to excavate a suppressed history that women could embrace and, perhaps more importantly, celebrate.

The pageant's structure, indeed, moves from abjection to celebration. At the beginning of the pageant, Prejudice holds Woman in figurative bondage as "a very child in the ways of the world, / a thing protected" (23), perhaps suggested by the literal bondage seen in Margetson's painting. She kneels at the feet of Justice and from that position she rises to defend herself when there is no one else to do so. Despite her abject position at the outset, she proves to be articulate, logical, and even poetic throughout and victorious at the end. Unlike the complex comic irony of Hamilton's other suffrage drama, the tone of *A Pageant of Great Women* is generally formal yet celebratory, and the pageant clearly ends on a jubilant note. Cockin points out that, at the premiere, Hamilton noted that Prejudice would "Exit in tears, with a despairing shriek, chased by Miss Chase" (1998: 100) as Joan of Arc, which suggests a giddy moment of triumph. Like many pageants, Hamilton's *Great Women* is aspirational and celebratory. At the end of the play, Woman imagines herself at dawn, a frequent revolutionary emblem, beginning an era of freedom and justice for women.

Unlike most pageants, *A Pageant of Great Women* was performed in purpose-built theatres or halls large enough to accommodate many performers and, organizers hoped, very large audiences. Beginning in September 1910, Craig took *A Pageant of Great Women* on tour: September 24 in Beckenham; October 3 in Middlesbrough; October 10 in Sunderland; October 15 in Sheffield; October 20 in Ipswich; October 26 in Cambridge; November 5 in Bristol; and finally a performance in London on November 18. After Craig formed the Pioneer Players, there were three subsequent performances in 1911 and 1912.

A well-designed, illustrated edition of *A Pageant of Great Women* and a "very limited large paper edition (numbered copies)"[13] as well as special pageant photographs and postcards were published by the Suffrage Shop in 1910. A second edition with a foreword by Hamilton appeared in 1948; it is widely anthologized and the full text is available online through Google Books. With a very large cast but only three speaking parts, *A Pageant of Great Women* must have been alluring to many suffrage groups that imagined that they might easily produce the pageant to benefit their organization. Other great women might easily be added to reflect the location of performance. This was certainly the case for the production in Cambridge on October 26, 1910. One heavily annotated script of *A Pageant of Great Women* in the Ellen Terry/Edith Craig Papers contains dialogue penciled in announcing "a group of noble dames," including Frances Sidney and Margaret Beaufort, which indicates that it was used for the performance in Cambridge's Guildhall. That script is filled with musical cues, including "Sappho music" and drumming for the Warrior group, indicative of a lively musical accompaniment throughout.[14]

Her *Pageant of Great Women* sought large stages. Included in the instructions for provincial productions is the stipulation that "It is necessary for it to be given in a large Hall [*sic*], with a large platform, or in a large garden." In staging the pageant, the great women might leave the stage to circulate among the audience effacing the time and space that separate them from the spectators. The best documented and described performance is the one discussed by Moran, not least because he includes a photograph of this production that shows the great women assembled on stage with their arms raised in a gesture of solidarity. Moran's analysis of the Swansea production in May 1910 reports that "the event concluded when the characters descended from the stage and marched around the hall before returning to the stage" (2017: 109), dissolving the barriers between the great women and the audience.

All of the productions of *A Pageant of Great Women* offered a more secure performance space than the many great suffrage processions beginning with the 1907 Mud March. The women who appeared in the pageant were not vulnerable to the mockery, abuse, and violence that suffragists encountered from the public and the police on the streets of London. Moreover, the audiences for the pageant were hardly typical theatre audiences. The suffrage orientation in the posters, advertisements, press releases, and programs was unmistakable. The audience's horizon of expectations anticipates both an affirmation of shared beliefs and an extravagant show. In the prewar period, Hamilton's and other suffrage plays advanced what were counter-hegemonic beliefs that today seem like obvious common sense: throughout history, women made important contributions outside the home; women should be free; women deserve equal justice under the law. Sponsored by suffragist groups, the pageant invited spectators to "come and realize your beliefs" (*Vote*, qtd. in Cockin 1998: 97). The *Times* review of the premiere recorded that "apparently the whole of the large audience were in enthusiastic sympathy with the movement."[15] As for so many pageants, the audience was not limited to adults. Advertisements in Liverpool reminded ticket-buyers that "juveniles must be paid"; for the matinee in Nottingham on May 4, 1911, children were admitted at a reduced ticket price.

Several scholars have commented on the display of women's bodies in *A Pageant of Great Women*. Outside of London, typically amateurs who were affiliated with sponsoring suffragist groups would perform the nonspeaking great women. Craig prepared casting notes that offered a general physical description of the amateurs to be cast as the great women, although these were guidelines rather than rules. Joan of Arc, for instance, is described as "tall, straight hair, very pretty" and in another version as "inspired looking—wear chain mail— tall," although at the premiere she was played by the petite Pauline Chase. In one draft of her casting notes, Craig stipulates that six of the ten Warriors, the only six among the entire cast, "must show legs,"[16] a potentially perilous immodesty in the day. Many commentators describe the Warriors as cross-dressing, but equally striking is the way in which the warrior women, as well as Rosa Bonheur, known for her advocacy of sensible dress and the character Craig always played, transgressed the WSPU's insistence on ladylike, "dainty and precise" dress. Both Holledge (1981) and Farkas (2019) locate the performance of amateurs in *A Pageant of Great Women* in what the former calls "the tradition of drawing-room amateur theatre, which dated from the late Victorian era" (1981: 72) and the latter describes as "genteel variety theatre."

Just as the amateur performers were on display, so were the costumes. Central to *A Pageant of Great Women* are the costumes appropriate to three allegorical figures and women from any time from the sixth century BC to 1909. Typical of most pageant productions in this decade, the organizers made much of the accuracy or authenticity of these costumes. In this instance, Edith Craig's long experience as a theatrical costumer and the research on several of the great women conducted by Lina Rathbone, who played one of the Warriors, made this more than just a hollow claim. The costumes were one of the most tightly controlled dimensions of the pageant. Hamilton notes that Craig "always provided the whole wardrobe" (1949: 42).[17] Craig explained: "It is usual to get the local ladies to undertake the various non-speaking character, and pay for the hire of their own dresses,"[18] which varied from 7s. 6d., to 10s., to 12s. for two successive performances or as much as five times the price of the most expensive ticket.

Additional great women appear in the pirated versions in produced in South Africa and Ireland, but in England, Craig and Hamilton successfully exerted strict control over *A Pageant of Great Women*. The text was copyrighted by Hamilton in England, but as advertised on the letterhead of the Pioneer Players, Craig acted as "sole agent" for it and more than a dozen other "Propaganda Plays," including George Bernard Shaw's *Press Cuttings* and Hamilton's *The Anti-Suffrage Waxworks* and *Jack and Jill and a Friend*.

With the performance rights came Craig's services (and fees) as director and her extensive inventory of costumes. Craig insisted on rehearsals for the amateurs who appeared as the great women. She prepared a prospectus that unambiguously asserted the conditions of production:

1. That I myself stage manage and produce at the performance.

2. That it is dressed according to my directions.

3. That the three speaking parts are played by professionals. (the other characters numbering from 53 to 72 as required can be played by amateurs.)

4. That a large enough hall or theatre is engaged.

5. That an orchestra is engaged (for which I will supply the music).

6. That you guarantee to pay the fees and travelling expense of the professionals concerned.

7. That your Society is responsible for getting together the cast, with the exception of the professionals—and for all the expenses incurred by the performance.

If you have seen the performance, you will realize that it is practically impossible to produce it adequately without professional assistance; and as I do not care to have it done ineffectively I am obliged to insist on superintending the rehearsals and performance.[19]

Like Parker, Craig exercised the discipline of a pageant-master. Craig's fees for the twelve performances in 1910 varied widely. In Cambridge, Craig's costs came to £32 15s. 5d. but for two performances in Sheffield in 1910, Craig billed £107 4s. (about £12,710 in 2020 prices).[20]

Despite what may seem to be the inflexibility of the terms that Hamilton and Craig insisted upon, *A Pageant of Great Women* was popular and profitable. The AFL's Secretary's Report (June 1909 to June 1910) records that the November 12, 1909 premiere "proved so successful financially that we were at last enabled to carry out a long cherished scheme and launch forth into offices."[21] For a much larger audience at the Royal Albert Hall on December 11, 1909, Ethel Smyth conducted the "March of the Women," which became the anthem of the suffrage campaign. Although she was not Smith's first choice to write the words,[22] Hamilton crafted the lyrics that returned to the trope of "dawn is breaking" to suit Smith's stirring music.

Including the tableaux performances, *A Pageant of Great Women* was performed more than twenty times between 1909 and 1912, including five times in London. The programs and publicity for several provincial productions note that profits would support the suffrage cause. *A Pageant of Great Women* is, at least in Britain, still in copyright with performance rights available from Samuel French for £39 plus VAT.

Comparing Emmeline Pankhurst to Hitler in 1935 has not endeared Hamilton to many feminist critics, but Hamilton was never doctrinaire. Her antipathy, even contempt, for the Pankhursts did not prevent her from allowing her pageant to be performed under the auspices of the WSPU in Bristol on November 5, 1910 and even taking the part of Woman. In 1920, she savagely portrayed the acolytes in the WSPU in her anti-war novel *William: An Englishman*, which won the first Femina Vie Heureuse prize.[23] Nor have Hamilton's reflections in *Life Errant* on her involvement in suffrage activism secured her a place in feminist hagiography:

Figure 6 *Cicely Hamilton as Mrs. Knox in the premiere of Shaw's* Fanny's First Play. *Original publication:* The Play Pictorial, *1911. Photo by Lena Connell/Hulton Archive/Getty Images.*

I never attempted to disguise the fact that I wasn't wildly interested in votes for anyone and ... if I worked for women's enfranchisement (and I did work quite hard) it wasn't because I hoped for great things from counting female noses at general elections, but because the agitation for women's enfranchisement must inevitably shake and weaken the tradition of the "normal woman". The "normal women" with her "destiny" of marriage and motherhood and housekeeping, no interest outside her home—especially no interest in the man's preserve of politics! My personal revolt was feminist rather than suffragist. (1935: 65)

Hamilton was involved in many of the 1910 productions of *A Pageant of Great Women*, but in April 1911 she played the pious Mrs. Knox in Shaw's *Fanny's First Play*, which opened at the Little Theatre in the Adelphi. Seen in character and photographed by Lena Connell (Figure 6), Hamilton was thirty-nine years old.

Afterlife

St. John's play *The First Actress*, first performed by Craig's Pioneer Players on May 8, 1911, employs a pageant dramaturgy not unlike *A Pageant of Great Women*. Here the great women, now all actors, appear in the dreams of Margaret Hughes, the first woman performer to appear on the English stage after the Restoration (Cockin 1998: 123). As Susan Carlson observes, *The First Actress* "becomes a pageant, then, as eleven famous actresses succeed one another in relating the future glory of women's stage presence" (2001: 342). Taking a longer perspective, Scott argues that

There is also a connection to be made here between the achievements of women in suffrage plays such as Hamilton's *A Pageant of Great Women* (1909) and Christopher St.

John's *The First Actress* (1911) and historical drama during
the interwar period. The popularity of the historical or
"bio" play in the 1920s and 1930s shows what Gale calls
the "the search for national heroines." (2013: 139)

The popularity of pageants made "pageant" an attractive
catchword in the century's second decade. For the matinee of
The Pageant of Shakespeare's Heroines at the New Princes'
Theatre February 9, 1912, Hamilton composed a humorous
prologue.[24] Like St. John's *The First Actress*, this pageant
employs dream visions: "Shakespeare is represented as
asleep and the heroines of his plays visit him in his dream,
all speaking a few lines from their most famous speeches."[25]
The organizations that Hamilton was most closely associated
with, the WWSL and the AFL, sponsored A *Pageant of Famous
Men and Women* at the Hotel Cecil on June 29, 1914, where
she appeared as George Eliot.[26] Within weeks, the outbreak
of the First World War reoriented Hamilton's and the nation's
priorities; Hamilton left England for France to work for the
Scottish ambulance service and, later, to form a repertory
company to entertain troops in France.

American Suffrage Pageants

Especially controversial was an attempt to stage Hamilton's
pageant in New York in the spring of 1911. On March 12,
1911, the *New York Times* reported:

It was the intention of those in charge of the benefit here
[including Carrie Chapman Catt] to reproduce [*A Pageant
of Great Women*], but Miss Hamilton made extraordinary
requests which could not be met. She demanded a guarantee
of fifty performances, a percentage of the gross receipts, and
a considerable sum in advance of royalties. Furthermore, she
wanted the pageant to be staged just as it was in London. ...

> It was found that all the great women in Miss Hamilton's
> pageant were Englishwomen, and that the American woman
> had been entirely ignored.... [this] caused the rejection of
> Miss Hamilton's pageant, and Mrs. Augusta Raymond
> Kidder was commissioned to write a strictly American
> pageant.[27]

An account published in the New York *Sun* described the
decision as "A new declaration of independence ... It is not the
tyranny of man from which the devotees of the cause are seeking
to emancipate themselves this time, but the sway of the English
suffragette."[28] There is much here that is grossly inaccurate
and more that reveals the differences between the US and
British suffrage movements. *A Pageant of Great Women* was
not focused on Englishwomen, let alone exclusively populated
by them. Rather than "fifty performances," fifty performers
may have been stipulated. The *Sun* article indicates that Craig,
rather than Hamilton, acted as "sole agent" by 1911 and set
these terms, not least because Hamilton was likely already in
rehearsals for *Fanny's First Play*.[29]

Just seventeen days after the rejection of Hamilton's
pageant, Augusta Kidder's all-American *The Pageant of Protest*
was staged at the Broadway Theatre. Kidder's 1911 pageant
was well-attended and well-received in a single performance
at a theatre that accommodated more than 2,000. Symbolic
characters, including the United States (later Uncle Sam),
Columbia, Enlightenment, the Average Man, and Indifference,
introduced historical tableaux of American women beginning
with the pioneers and moving through history. Featured were
the likes of Betsy Ross, Mary Baker Eddy, Julia Ward Howe,
and Susan B. Anthony. Although superficially indebted to
Hamilton's pageant, Kidder's *Pageant of Protest*, the forerunner
to her 1915 pageant, *Uncle Sam's Daughters and What They
Have Done*, displays the blinkered patriotism that vindicates
Hamilton's and Craig's reluctance to relinquish control of *A
Pageant of Great Women*.

With roots in nineteenth-century social protest, specifically anti-slavery activism and the temperance crusade, the American suffrage movement was also attracted to pageantry, largely as transmitted by Alice Paul and Lucy Burns. After 1905, when the central offices of the WSPU relocated from Manchester to London, the British movement was more centralized than the American, although most of the American pageants were staged in either Washington or New York City. The American movement was geographically decentralized because before 1914 the campaign of the National Woman Suffrage Association concentrated on securing women's enfranchisement on a state-by-state rather than national basis. Indeed, women had full voting rights in all of the Western US states as well as South Dakota, Kansas, Oklahoma, Michigan, and New York before the ratification of the Nineteenth Amendment to the US Constitution in 1920. Whereas the British suffrage movement attracted and incorporated artists, actors, musicians, and writers through organizations founded in the first decade of the twentieth century, the American movement was more dependent not only on small cadres of well-educated women, often from the "seven sisters" or other elite schools, but also on patronage from very wealthy women. Less conspicuous in the American suffrage movement is the close collaboration with artists—costume designers, painters, the Arts and Crafts artists, professional actors—before 1914. An eBay search for suffrage jewelry from the prewar period shows that more than 90 percent of it is in the UK. There are many striking images from the American suffrage movement, to be sure, but those of the British campaign depict a more fully developed iconography. The American movement styled itself as intensely patriotic, even all-American. As the American suffrage imagery developed in the second decade of the century, the US parades and processions feature generically patriotic American flags or bunting that would not be out of place on the Fourth of July. Susan Ware writes that "open-air suffrage parades and pageants were both still quite unusual [in the United States] in 1913" (2019: 201). Indeed, even after 1913, the women's suffrage movement strove to present a nonpartisan appeal to US patriotism. The American suffrage pageants are usually allegorical or all-American, whereas Hamilton's not only crossed national borders, but also moved through centuries of distinguished women.

The most prolific creator of American suffrage pageants was Hazel MacKaye, sister of Percy, who saw the idiom as a vehicle for agit-prop: "a pageant has more power to convince people of the truth of our cause than any other means. A pageant is a forceful and vivid form of drama" (1914b: 6). On March 3, 1913, a *Woman Suffrage Allegory and Pageant Parade* by Hazel MacKaye and Elmira L. Tinnen was performed on the steps of the Treasury Building in Washington, DC. Having returned from their apprenticeship with the Pankhursts in the UK, Alice Paul and Lucy Burns organized the Women's Suffrage Procession that was staged on the eve of Woodrow Wilson's inauguration as president. As often in the United States, this suffrage pageant was a top-down project for which Paul and Barnes raised "over $27,000, much of it from restless women of wealth" (Dubois 2020: 189). The pageant, which involved about thirty performers and no dialogue, hired choreographer and dancer Florence Fleming Noyes, opera singer and actor Hedwiga Reicher, and other professionals to appear as Liberty, Columbia (the personification of the nation), Justice, Charity, Peace, and Hope, allegorical figures that would become familiar in American suffrage pageants.[30] Karen J. Blair describes the *Woman Suffrage Allegory* as affirming "women's special qualities by representing them as symbolic Greek figures from antiquity" (1990: 23).

The plan was that the pageant would begin at the Treasury Building at the same time that the parade stepped off fourteen blocks away and that the pageant performers would join with the marchers at the Treasury Building: "the group [pageant performers] would review—and then join—the parade marchers, the foot-soldiers of the suffrage cause" (Roberts 2017: 17). Unfortunately, it was a cool day, with a high in the fifties. The marchers did not begin on time and then encountered intense heckling that devolved into assaults that injured 200 marchers and sent 100 of them to the hospital. Pageant performers waited on the granite steps of Treasury Building in their diaphanous costumes, but retreated indoors before the marchers arrived (Roberts 2017: 18). Nonetheless, Madsen argues that "MacKaye gave the day's myriad, moving parts an overarching narrative, dramatizing its purpose" (2014: 284).

On May 2, 1913, another American suffrage pageant was staged before a packed house at the Metropolitan Opera House in New York City as part of a program that featured the first suffrage address by former president Theodore Roosevelt. *A Dream of Freedom*, written by Margaret Merriam Tuttle, perhaps closer to a ballet than a pageant, was performed to music and, like *Woman Suffrage Allegory*, without dialogue. Several commentators described *A Dream of Freedom* as "short and beautiful" interlude or, in the words of Katharine Lord, "strictly speaking, a symbolic pantomime, rather than a pageant."[31]

There was a flurry of American suffrage pageants in 1914, many of which depicted women as victims. The most Parkerian of them, Hazel MacKaye's *The American Woman: Six Periods of American Life*, was staged on April 17, 1914 at the 69th Street Armory in New York City. The foreword to its program observes that "Since the history of humanity [*sic*], men and women have been working side by side—equally sharing the burdens of life—equally useful and equally necessary to the community and to the upbuilding of civilization." The first scenes show a Native American chief who "sells his daughter to secure the much-coveted [bison] pelt" and "an old and revered resident" of Salem unfairly accused of witchcraft and denied a fair trial.[32] As plainly indebted to Parker's pageants as this one was, its last two episodes portray the present leadership of the suffragettes and, using the allegorical figures of Justice, Man, Woman, and the Spirit of Triumph, a future when "the light reveals The Prophecy of the Future in which Justice is fulfilled" (1914a: n.p.). In Blair's assessment, Hazel MacKaye "succeeded in portraying a history of American sexism too bald and brutal to win acceptance. ... the script was biting, not subtle, and bared centuries of sexism endured by American women ... certainly no pageant before this one had presented so radical an analysis of a controversial matter" (1990: 25). Although Blair's statement may be accurate in regards to American suffrage pageants, earlier counter-hegemonic pageants in Ireland and Hamilton's had edges just as sharp.

In December 1915, Hazel MacKaye's celebratory *Susan B. Anthony*, with 18 speaking roles, 400 supporting players, and 625 costumes, was staged for a single performance in Washington by the Congressional Union for Woman Suffrage for the 47th annual convention of the National Suffrage Association. "Interspersed throughout the [ten] episodes were four symbolic 'friezes.' Filling a shallow 'lunette' above the stage proper were ten young girls in classic costumes, whose grouping and attitudes symbolized at appropriate intervals throughout the scenes, 'Women's Despair,' 'Women's Unity,' 'The Dawn of Hope,' and, finally, 'Onward, Glorious Soldiers'."[33] Blair reports that "MacKaye's pageant deifying Susan B. Anthony achieved all its aims. It enraptured the audience of three thousand legislators, society people of influence, and suffragists at Convention Hall" (1990: 41). Pageants became a regular feature in Anthony's many commemorations. A "dance drama" to "show the progress of women" in eleven episodes, for instance, was created by Jean Wold and performed in July 1923 in Seneca Falls, NY.[34] Another pageant tribute to Susan B. Anthony, *Woman Awakened*, was performed by the Seneca Falls Centennial Committee in 1948.

With the exception of Hazel MacKaye's *The American Woman: Six Periods of American Life* and *Susan B. Anthony*, the American suffrage pageants moved away from historical episodes and into allegorical abstractions, suggesting how closely pageant and masque were linked in American suffrage drama. In the United States, suffrage pageants retain the all-American qualities of Kidder's 1911 *The Pageant of Protest* and gesture toward a transnational vision only obliquely, if at all. They also consistently articulate the argument for suffrage from an overtly patriotic posture, rendering them a hybrid of hegemonic and counter-hegemonic. Often, the American pageants celebrate woman as mother, often through abstract figures such as Maternity or Motherhood, in a way that Hamilton plainly did not. Nor did Hamilton's pageant foreground feminine beauty, victimhood, or domesticity.

Pirated Pageants

Hamilton's *A Pageant of Great Women* was staged twice by South Africa's Women's Reform Club in May 1911 at His Majesty's Theatre in Johannesburg. Photographs of those productions show costumes that, while detailed, are not those created by Craig and used in the English productions. Along with the Voortrekkers and Dutch-speaking settlers, this iteration portrays Olive Schreiner (1890–1980), the South African judge and anti-war activist who was herself a member of the WWSL that Hamilton founded. Charlotte Corday appears, oddly, with a rifle. The pageant's artistic director was George Salisbury Smithers (1873–1919), a graduate of the Slade School. The pageant was so well-received and popular that it "enabled the Club to close the year with a balance of £29."[35] No evidence of royalties paid to Hamilton has been unearthed.

On May 24, 1913, another pirated production of Hamilton's *A Pageant of Great Women* was performed outdoors before an audience of 500 in Wynnewood (suburban Philadelphia), Pennsylvania by the College Club of Philadelphia. The famous women of Hamilton's pageant may have been replaced by an all-America group, but the play's structure and dialogue were retained. The next day, the *Philadelphia Inquirer* printed a very favorable report and no fewer than twelve full lines *verbatim* from Hamilton's pageant.[36] On October 6, 1913, the *Inquirer* reported that the Equal Franchise League performed another revival of the pageant, now authored by "Lady Cicely Hamilton."[37] In 1923, the title was used in Buffalo by the New York State Federation of Women's Club.

Cockin details a failed attempt to stage *A Pageant of Great Women* for the Seventh International Woman Suffrage Congress in Hungary in 1913. Hamilton herself corresponded with Countess Iska Teleki to express "no objection to changing the characters, even a suggestion that the substitution proved the international relevance of the play" (qtd. in Cockin 1998: 102). Although these plans fell through, Hamilton clearly saw that her pageant might well accommodate other great women as had been the case for the performance in Cambridge.

Just after Easter in 1914 and only three months after the end of the Dublin Lockout, the Irish Women's Franchise League staged the Daffodil Fete which employed a format familiar in both Ireland and England that combined tableaux vivants, addresses, recitations, and musical interludes by women performers. Like the British productions, there was music, provided in Dublin by Miss McGrane's ladies trio. Its centerpiece was two evening dramatic performances: the premiere of the one-act comedy of Francis Sheehy-Skeffington's *The Prodigal Daughter* and an Irish adaptation of *A Pageant of Great Women*. Many of the best-known performers in Dublin took roles in *A Pageant of Great Women*: Madame Daisy Bannard Cogley appeared as Sappho; Elizabeth Young played Deirdre; Mrs. McDonagh appeared as Maeve; St. Brigid was impersonated by Maire Walker [nic Shuibhlaigh]. Molesworth Hall was a much smaller venue than those that hosted the pageant in England and the number of great women in Dublin was probably less than a quarter of those in the Scala Theatre premiere. Four of the tableaux featured Joan of Arcs, the most popular of the great women. At least two specifically Irish tableaux were adduced for the Dublin production. In one, thuggish British soldiers manhandle the Irish republican Anne Devlin (1780–1851). In the second, a fully armored Joan of Arc (played by the first woman elected to Parliament, Constance Markievicz) releases the Irish suffragist prisoner

(Kathryn Houston). The pageant producers did not want for ingenuity: Markievicz's impressive suit of armor was actually made of linoleum.

In England, the First World War nearly extinguished pageants as a popular theatrical form. All of the major suffrage organizations in the UK withdrew from activism in support of the war effort. When pageants did appear after Britain's entry into war in August 1914, they were staged in support of the war effort. Gladys Davidson created *Britannia's Revue* (1914) for music hall performance and, in 1919, *Britannia's Pageant of Peace*. The *Pageant of Women*, staged outdoors in London on Saturday, July 17, 1915, included "Belgium, impersonated by a stately woman clad in purple and black bearing a tattered flag" and other women as symbolic representatives of the Allied Nations.[38] In 1917, the Lord Chamberlain licensed Louis Napoleon Parker's *A Pageant of Fair Women*, which was performed on May 8, 1917 as part of the Joan of Arc Day festivities. Clara Butt appeared as the "spirit of the Empire," David Lloyd George's daughter Olwen appeared as Wales, with others representing the Allied nations.[39] Although Hamilton never wrote another pageant, Craig periodically produced pageants, including a *Pageant of Tenterden* in July 1935 that celebrated the village near Ellen Terry's home where Craig lived with Christopher St. John until their deaths (Craig's in 1947 and St. John's in 1960).

3

Pageant as Mega-Event: *Isles of Wonder*

In the mid-to-late nineteenth century, pageants appeared in the programming of a number of exhibitions that sought not merely local or national audiences, but international ones. Like most pageants, these were celebratory hegemonic spectacles that often took "progress" as their theme. In an age of growing mobility and immigration, industrialization, and enfranchisement, these events hoped not only to showcase a nation's strengths and accomplishments, but also to forge a bond, however transitory or illusory, among increasingly large and diverse populations. In France, a series of national expositions preceded the French Industrial Exposition in 1844. The landmark in the exhibition movement, the Great Exhibition of Britain in 1851, for which the Crystal Palace was constructed in Hyde Park, is often credited with triggering the international exposition or world's fair movement. John J. MacAloon describes the 1851 Great Exhibition as "the first truly international exhibition, whose mass popularity (over six million visitors), coherent embodiment of Victorian culture, and determined ideology of industrial and moral progress made it the model which all subsequent universal expositions, including the French, strove to emulate" (2008: 148). For the 1893 Chicago World's Columbian Exposition, commemorating the anniversary of Columbus's 1492 excursion to North America, celebrated artists, architects, painters, musicians, and inventors created the temporary Great White City as well as more enduring contributions such as Pabst Blue Ribbon beer, the Ferris wheel, and Frederick Jackson Turner's frontier thesis. By 1899, the industrial exposition and world's fair movement had its own journal: *The World's Work*. In this climate, Pierre de Coubertin spearheaded a campaign to revitalize the Olympic Games. Not unlike the international expositions, the Olympics appealed to citizens who had not only mobility, but also leisure time and the price of a ticket.

Coubertin saw the Olympics much as Parker saw pageants; they certainly drew on similar sources of inspiration. As Fischer-Lichte notes, after Coubertin's visit to the Bayreuth Festival, "it was Wagner's *Gesamtkunstwerk* which inspired the idea of the great festival of the Olympic Games" (2005: 74). Like the American pageant movement, Coubertin believed that such projects could create the meaningful leisure that bettered ordinary lives as well as society at large; they could also produce physically fit, disciplined military recruits. Coubertin went much further in believing that the Olympics could offer a new, substitute religion to promote world peace and to mitigate "the moral disorder produced by the discoveries of industrial science" (qtd. in MacAloon 2008: 209). As a new religion might, the Olympics invented and then institutionalized an ever-expanding series of ceremonies and rituals. There would be a symbol—one that reflected the Games' global reach and that would become universally recognizable: five rings representing the five continents. There would also be a flag, an anthem, all copyrighted and vigilantly protected from apostatic appropriation, so that they could later be commodified and marketed. Its name would be capitalized. To evangelize Coubertin's Olympism, powerful hierarchical structures controlled every aspect of the Games.

The Olympic movement proclaimed itself a progressive, global movement that celebrated human achievement but simultaneously placed great emphasis on competition among nations. It brought together political entities that viewed one another as enemies to compete with respect and bonhomie on what was imagined to be a level playing field. It offered individuals marginalized or vilified by hegemonic forces the opportunity to distinguish themselves on an international stage. Indeed, many of the popular films and television series about the Olympics, such as *Chariots of Fire* (Hudson, 1981) or *The Jesse Owens Story* (Irving, 1981), revel in the international success of people mocked and derided for their religion or race. The Olympics aspired to create a utopian community of wonderfully fit, healthy, usually young people doing things they did very well to the delight of the general public—a fantasy of what modern life could be.

That model, however, is very tightly controlled in every way by the International Olympic Committee (IOC). For the Games, the IOC mandates an opening ceremony with two basic components: required Olympic protocols and artistic elements. The former are the "rituals" required by the IOC and the IPC (International Paralympic Committee). The protocol elements in the opening ceremony include the entry of the head of state, the playing the national anthem, the parade of the athletes, the symbolic release of doves (disastrously roasted in the Olympic flame in Seoul in 1988), the opening of the Games by the head of state, the raising of the Olympic flag, the playing of the Olympic anthem, Olympic oaths taken first by an athlete, then by an official, then by a coach, the torch relay, and the lighting of an Olympic cauldron. The fifth element specifies the exact words that the head of state is permitted to speak and limits what may be said to those words alone. At the opening of the 1936 Olympic Games in Berlin, even Adolf Hitler complied. Some of these IOC protocols or rituals have existed since the Games were revitalized in 1896, but the IOC continues to tweak and to elaborate them, just as it continues to extend its control over every aspect of the Olympics. The Olympic flag was not hoisted until 1920. Berlin saw the first torch relay in 1936. The IOC controls the opening ceremonies as much as any authority—Church, State, or censor—ever controlled a pageant.

Olympic Bids

In the throes of a global economic depression, Los Angeles was the only city to bid for the 1932 Games. The IOC's successful commodification of the Games, specifically when the Games were again held in Los Angeles in 1984 (see Hogan 2003; D'Agati 2011), fueled competition to host the Games. So great are the prestige and the perceived economic advantages in hosting the Olympics that, despite the ever-increasing IOC demands and staggering costs, competition among host cities intensified in the late twentieth century. The formulation of the London bid for the 2012 Games was well underway by June 2003, when Barbara Cassani was appointed to lead London's bid committee. Sebastian Coe, who won four Olympic medals at the Games in Moscow (1980) and Los Angeles (1984), took over from Cassani in May 2004. To great jubilation in the UK, the IOC awarded London the 2012 Summer Games on July 6, 2005, the day before 56 people were killed and 784 wounded in the "7/7" terrorist bombings in London.

Opposition to hosting the Games has resulted in recent vigorous (and effective) community activism. When Oslo dropped out of the bidding for the 2022 Winter Olympics, Norwegian media described the IOC as a "notoriously ridiculous organization run by grifters and hereditary aristocrats" (Mathis-Lilley 2014) that demanded minibars stocked with Coca-Cola products, meeting rooms kept at exactly 20 degrees Celsius and a bevy of other concessions. In 2015, when Boston was designated as one of the US cities authorized to prepare a bid to host the 2024 summer Olympics, opposition quickly coalesced around the organization No Boston Olympics. That organization's website offered this description of the IOC:

> The International Olympic Committee (IOC) is an unelected, private organization headquartered in Lausanne, Switzerland, where it takes advantage of lower tax rates and lax oversight. The IOC requires host cities to agree to a set of lavish demands, including a ceremonial welcome on the

airport runway and complimentary luxury accommodations that include "seasonal fruits and cakes." The IOC's members will have immense impact over Greater Boston's future. ... Among the IOC's demands is a requirement that host governments reserve lanes on public highways for the exclusive use of the IOC. Boston 2024 is proposing that federal taxpayers pay for private chauffeurs and the operation of these lanes: so not only will Massachusetts residents be sitting in traffic, they will be paying for the IOC members to avoid it![1]

No Boston Olympics successfully extricated Boston from formulating a bid; the 2024 Games eventually went to Paris.

The success of the London bid led to the formation of the London Organising Committee for the Olympic Games (LOCOG), chaired by Coe. For the next seven years, LOCOG negotiated with community, city, and national authorities as well as a very wide variety of private sector groups to fulfill IOC criteria and sustain support for the Games among Britons. For the 2012 London games, in addition to the stadia, facilities, and corporate sponsorship:

The IOC required that LOCOG set aside 250 miles of VIP lanes for exclusive use by members of the Olympic family, to secure nearly 2,000 rooms for IOC bigwigs and associates in the finest five-star hotels, and to control commercial space in support of Olympic sponsors. In particular, the IOC's *Technical Manual on Brand Protection* stipulates that "candidate cities are required to obtain control of all billboard advertising, city transport advertising, airport advertising, etc. for the duration of the games and the month preceding the games to support the marketing program." (Zimbalist 2015: 109–10)

As did the Lord Chamberlain before 1968, the IOC required that the host city submit the script and plans for the opening ceremony months in advance for its written approval.

The Olympic Charter has always stipulated an opening ceremony to accommodate official protocol elements, but the elaboration of the "artistic segments" is a fairly recent development. The Depression took a heavy toll on the number of countries participating, with only thirty-nine in the 1932 Los Angeles Games, down from forty-six in the 1928 games. There was an opening ceremony, but without the head of state, President Herbert Hoover (who sent Vice-President Charles Curtis), and without the pageant of national identity that later evolved. The *New York Times* described the Los Angeles opening ceremony as "the roar of cannon, the crashing of bands and the liberation of thousands of pigeons."[2]

Maurice Roche writes that the "organisation and staging [of the 1936 Berlin Games] far outstripped all previous Olympic events" (2000: 113). Recognizing the propaganda value of its lavish spectacles, the Third Reich commissioned Leni Riefenstahl to film the Berlin games as newly mandated by the IOC.[3] The IOC expected documentation of the competitions; what they got was Riefenstahl's two-part masterpiece of propaganda: *Olympia* (1938). Only sixteen months after the release of her *Triumph of the Will*, Riefenstahl used multiple cameras, some attached to balloons, to film the opening ceremony on August 1, 1936. To memorialize the first Olympic torch relay, her film prefaces footage of the Berlin Games with a twenty-minute fantasia that begins in the ruins of Greece and celebrates, as Riefenstahl so often does, the ideal human form—here seen in classical statuary and living performers. The torch is carried along the sea and through hillside villages, from Greece to Bulgaria, Yugoslavia, Hungary, Austria, Czechoslovakia, and finally Germany. Riefenstahl moves then to the massive columns of Berlin's newly constructed Olympiastadion, filled to its capacity of 100,000. Hitler is a very real presence throughout her film. During the march of the athletes, not only the German athletes, but also those from Austria, Italy, and France return Hitler's Nazi salute. His declaration of the opening of the Games are the first words heard in her film.[4] After the Olympic flag is raised and doves are released, Riefenstahl returns to the journey of the Olympic torch as cheering crowds mob the highly decorated Charlottenburger Chausee before the Brandenburg Gate. Berlin seems untouched by economic depression, a beautiful European capital in full flower. Carried by a tall blond runner who personifies Hitler's ideal human physiognomy, the torch lights the cauldron and the athletes take their oaths. Although Hitler is a strong presence cheering every German victory, the remaining three hours of *Olympia* focuses on the athletic competitions themselves, including Jesse Owens's four gold medals. Riefenstahl's film not only won many awards, including best film at the 1938 Venice Film Festival and a gold medal from the IOC in 1939, but also proved financially profitable.

The Montreal Summer Games in 1976 significantly expanded the opening ceremonies to include traditional folk dancing and musical performances as well as military displays such as cannon fire and fly-overs. In Moscow in 1980, a further expansion of the spectacle with traditional dance and music, gymnastic and trampoline demonstrations, and a greeting from the Salyut 6 crew then in orbit high above the globe. Fireworks came to replace cannon fire. Jackie Hogan points out that, since the financial success of the heavily commercialized games in Los Angeles in 1984, "Games organizers have incorporated Hollywood-style opening and closing ceremonies into their Olympic program and adjusted the timing and structure of events to maximize global viewership" (2003: 103). In Barcelona in 1992, for instance, representations of Spanish and Catalan cultures dominate the much-expanded artistic segments using, for instance, flamenco dance and music, massed performers in the Catalan national colors, and figures that allude to Dali, Picasso, and Miro. In the first artistic segment that might be called a pageant for its use of personation to enact a historical narrative, a huge ship celebrated Barcelona's historical importance as an international seaport (see Hargreaves 2000: 101–3). Four years later, in Atlanta, one pageant episode featured neither high, folk, nor traditional but pop culture as young people performed a typical Saturday night out at an

American football game with dance teams, pick-up trucks, and cheerleaders. A second pageant episode personated historical figures to offer a highly sanitized version of the "Old South," remarkable for its willingness to gloss over the South's racist past. In the twenty-first century, the opening ceremonies did not merely incorporate interludes of entertainment that gestured toward local, native, or folkloric customs, but created bombastic pageants of national identity and the host nation's contributions to global culture.

Since the 2000 Olympics in Sydney, the opening ceremonies have gone far beyond the official Olympic protocols. On September 15, 2000, the Sydney opening ceremony included a fantasia celebrating the Great Barrier Reef, Aboriginal cultures, nature, and multiculturalism to chart Australia's evolution as a vibrant, modern culture. The 120 stockmen on horseback rode into the stadium, each carrying the Olympic and then the Australian flags, celebrating the outback heritage. Sequences depicting "Deep Blue Sea" and bushfires employed spectacular lighting and pyrotechnics to celebrate Australia's unique natural environment. A fanfare led by James Morrison, Julie Anthony, and the Sydney Symphony Orchestra heralded a waterfall that cascaded into a pool out of which arose an enormous cauldron that held the Olympic flame. D'Agati describes the Sydney opening ceremony as depicting the merger of "two separate culture: White/Western and Aboriginal … the most interesting moment comes during their convergence" (2011: 100).

The opening ceremony in Sydney was replete with allusions and in-jokes that privileged those who knew Australia. Helen Lenskyj reports that "many international audiences and media were indeed bewildered by symbols such as lawn mowers, outdoor toilets, and zinc cream, and a Japanese viewer complained that parts of the ceremony were 'a complete mystery'" (2002: 220). Nonetheless, Simon Anholt reports that "it is no exaggeration to say that the modern image of Sydney was built on the Opera House and the Olympic Games, and in consequence much of the high equity of Brand Australia (in

2005 the No. 1 country in Q2 of the Nation Brands Index)"
(2007: 108). The opening ceremony for the Athens games in
2004, which involved less technology and fewer performers,
celebrated the Greek heritage in moving friezes that recreated
and celebrated images of the human form from classical Greek
statuary, pottery, and paintings. Then came Beijing in 2008.

The Beautiful Olympics: "Brilliant Civilization" and "Glorious Era"

China's bid for the Olympics was an exercise in rebranding
the country to show that it had remedied its dire human rights
record by earning the IOC's approval. Lee points out that
China's earlier Olympic bid in 1993 was rejected "due to its
rule of Tibet and issues of human rights, political dissidents,
democracy and its relationship with Taiwan" (2010: 209). Only
after "China signed the United Nations Convention on Civil
and Political Rights that guarantees freedom of expression, a
fair trial and protection against torture and arbitrary arrest,"
Lee writes (209), did the IOC award Beijing the 2008 games.
She implies that China signed the UN convention partly, if not
expressly, to secure its bid for the Olympic Games.

The opening ceremony in 2008 was a pageant intended
to revise many of the negative perceptions of China. In the
United States, National Public Radio reported, "China's
image in the world may be changed by these games. At
least, that's what organizers and Communist Party officials
are hoping."[5] Like the 1936 Olympics in Berlin, the Beijing
Olympics, especially its opening ceremony was very tightly
controlled by the government to project the positive image
of a strong, prosperous nation. As in 2012, a filmmaker,
Zhang Yimou, best known for his CGI-dense action films
Raise the Red Lantern (1991) and *House of Flying Daggers*
(2004), staged the opening ceremony, which includes a short
film on paper-making.

The opening ceremony of the 2008 Beijing games may stand as the pinnacle of mass precision choreography for some time. The first act of the pageant, "Brilliant Civilization," was a spectacular representation of the Four Great Chinese Inventions (the compass, gunpowder, paper, and movable type) as well as displays of Chinese art forms—opera, scroll painting, puppetry, porcelain, music, ballet as well as martial arts and gymnastics. The second act, "Glorious Era," refers to the modern nation chosen by the IOC to host the Games. The performance of the artistic segments (i.e., the non-protocol events) occupied about one of the four hours of the ceremony.

It is difficult to overstate how positive the reception of Beijing's opening ceremony was. Reuters headlined its story on the response "World Media Hails [sic] Beijing's Perfect Night" (Ruwitch 2008). The costumes, choreography, visual spectacle, special effects (including acrobats performing on a huge glowing sphere suspended in the National Stadium), remain unsurpassed. So were the controversies that lingered after the ceremony: performers who were injured, crippled in fact, during rehearsals; the use of lip-syncing; children who appeared in ethnic-minority costume who were not members of that ethnic minority; the use of CGI in the ceremony's broadcast transmission. Some in the West thought that only a totalitarian state could produce such a spectacle. "What kind of society is it," asked Anthony Lane in the *New Yorker*, "that can afford to make patterns out of its people?" (2012: 28). Indeed, Zhang Yimou would "claim, perhaps with a measure of ironic pride, that only North Korea could have outdone his display of coordinated mass movement" (Barmé 2009: 71).

London 2012

Staging a pageant in a stadium that seated 80,000 people and would be seen by 900 million people in its initial television broadcast was perhaps less daunting than developing the artistic elements that would avoid derision and discord in an age of social media. The London bid to host the 2012 Olympic Games was developed in the first years of the new century when the British prime minister and mayor of London were both members of the Labour Party. By 2012, both Tony Blair and Ken Livingstone were out of office; in their places near the Queen in the new Olympic Stadium on July 23, 2012 were two Conservative successors: David Cameron and Boris Johnson. Although the extreme divisiveness of Brexit was still in the future, in 2012 Britain was deeply riven by economic recession and planned cuts to government spending, the terrorist bombings of July 7, 2005, the police killing of Mark Duggan in 2011 and subsequent riots.

In advance of 2012 opening ceremony, British commentators were dubious about matching let alone surpassing the success of the Beijing opening. "And since Beijing in 2008," wrote the LOCOG chairman, Sebastian Coe, "the view from the Clapham omnibus was, 'how can we top that?'" (2013: 436). Since the marriage of Prince Charles and Diana Spencer and certainly from the time of Diana's funeral, live broadcast spectaculars from Britain enjoyed immense global popularity. Only fifteen months before *Isles of Wonder*, tens of millions watched or live-streamed the wedding of Prince William and Kate Middleton. Well into the twenty-first century, Britain, the world judged, excelled in performing if not inventing such traditions.

Pageants, especially hegemonic ones endorsed or supported by the state that claim to represent an entire city, let alone nation, aspire to build consensus. Success would mean not only staging an opening ceremony to rival Beijing's, but also constructing a pageant of the British past and present that could generate consensus, perhaps even *communitas*. Shortly after the success of London's bid for the Olympics, Boyle told Coe that he had "lived in east London for twenty-five years and I can't wait to see the sport" (qtd. in Coe 2013: 437). Coe writes that from the early stages of planning Boyle "wanted to make both the TV and stadium experience more multimedia, and especially, he wanted to involve the spectators" (437). Mark Browning writes of the "celebratory, self-affirming tone" of Boyle's films: "he seems always to opt for the positive over the negative" (2012: 8). Boyle's experience with theatre, television, and film as well as media industries, his eye for the life-affirming, and his enthusiasm, made him a likely candidate to devise the opening ceremony. Having worked or studied in Scotland, Northern Ireland, and Wales and then living in England, Boyle had credentials that allowed him to speak for the "four countries" of the UK as well as the boroughs of East London. The final dance sequence of *Slumdog Millionaire*, in which hundreds of jubilant teenagers dance on a train platform to A. R. Rahman's "Jai Ho," might have been his demo reel. To undertake what Richard Williams (2012) in the *Guardian* called "the most thankless task in show business," the LOCOG named Danny Boyle as the artistic director of the opening ceremony in 2010.

Boyle's film work is his best known, but he began in theatre in the early 1980s with the Joint Stock Theatre Company, the Royal Court Theatre, and the Royal Shakespeare Company. By the late 1980s, he was in Northern Ireland directing television scripts based on work by Frank McGuinness and John McGahern. Since his first film, *Shallow Grave* (1994), Boyle has directed a steady output of fifteen feature films in twenty-six years. His big budget projects, such as directing Leonardo DiCaprio in *The Beach* (2000) and the James Bond film *No Time to Die* (Fukunaga [who replaced Boyle], not yet released), are among his least successful. *Trainspotting* (1996) was made for only £1 million. Even *Slumdog Millionaire*, which won the Oscar for Best Picture, had a very modest budget of $20 million.

Boyle's films typically deal with young people at the margins of society: the junkies of suburban Edinburgh in *Trainspotting*; a young soldier in a plague-ridden England in *28 Days Later* (2002); a nine-year-old boy isolated by grief over his mother's death in *Millions* (2004); a quick-witted Mumbai slum boy in *Slumdog Millionaire*; the struggling singer in a sleepy Suffolk town in *Yesterday* (2019). Grounded in recognizable contemporary settings, his films' landscapes are often defamiliarized by dream/fantasy sequences, intrusive cinematic techniques (especially fast-motion and flashbacks), or absence. The film *28 Days Later*, for instance, shows London eerily emptied, devoid of people and movement. The horrors of this dystopian thriller are matched by the nightmares that edge into his other films. The viewer is routinely unbalanced, never certain what is real or imagined, as *Trance* (2013) moves seamlessly in and out of sequences induced by hypnosis. Several films rely on a fantastic premise. *Millions* imagines the day when the UK enters a currency alliance with the EU that renders the British pound worthless. *Yesterday* is predicated on the premise that no one has ever heard a Beatles song. As familiar as his film worlds may be, Boyle has pursued these departures from reality to engage the audience's imagination by asking, "what if?" He often uses flashbacks, time-lapse, and fast motion cinematography, which often carries a meta-cinematic wink and nod. Even in these fantasy or alternative worlds, his characters face gritty realities. As Keith Hopper commented in a 1996 interview with Boyle, the genius of *Trainspotting* is how it "resists the traditional, moralistic demands of social realism in favor of a blackly comic surrealism" (1996: 11).

Another of Boyle's trademarks is his use of music to counterpoint image. In *Trainspotting*, excerpts from Bizet's *Carmen* play as Renton (Ewan McGregor) plunges down a filthy toilet to retrieve his drugs. Later, Lou Reed's "Perfect Day" is heard as Renton injects heroin, is seen to fall through the floor, is dumped at a hospital where he is revived then carried back to his boyhood bed in his parents' home.[6] Speaking more generally, Boyle has stated his larger creative inspiration is his love of music: "My biggest influence is music. That's my biggest single influence" (Boyle qtd. in Dunham 2011: xi).

Team Boyle

There are clear lines of continuity with writers, actors, and creative personnel in Boyle's earlier work who contributed to *Isles of Wonder*. Boyce's earlier collaboration with Boyle, *Millions*, remains one of Boyle's favorite films (Boyle 2013: 43). Boyce also had extensive experience as a writer for film and television, including the long-running British soap operas *Brookside* and *Coronation Street*. In 2011, Boyce revitalized Ian Fleming's *Chitty Chitty Bang Bang* (1964) to create a popular series of children's books. Especially important are the many collaborators who worked with Boyle on both the National Theatre production of *Frankenstein* (which opened in 2011) and *Isles of Wonder*:

> When I was approached about the opening ceremony ... I said my only commitment was to direct *Frankenstein* at the National. By the time I started on *Frankenstein*, I was already working with production designer Mark Tildesley, costume designer Suttirat Larlarb and writer Frank Cottrell Boyce. Mark and Suttirat came with me to the National as they both had experience in theatre, and I used *Frankenstein* as a dry run for composers Rick Smith and Karl Hyde from Underworld. ... Toby Sedgwick [movement director] was also a great influence on both jobs. (Boyle 2013: 363)

When Boyle was first chosen to direct *Frankenstein* for the National Theatre, Boyce gave him a copy of Humphrey Jennings's *Pandaemonium: 1660–1886*. Jennings, a founder of Mass Observation, celebrated documentarian, and polymath, created moving wartime documentaries, such as *Heart of Britain* (1941) and *Listen to Britain* (1942). These short films retain their emotive power because they feature ordinary people—miners, factory workers, clerks, men and women, old and young, at work and leisure. These films portray Britain's national identity as a rich composite of many entities, a civic society in which everyone plays a vital part. In an age of identity politics grounded in exclusionary considerations of racial, sexual, political, and cultural orientations, consensus seemed improbable if not impossible. That *Isles of Wonder* could configure Britain's identity in 2012 in a similar way is Boyle's perhaps signature achievement.

In *Pandaemonium: 1660–1886*, Jennings culled the hundreds of responses to "the coming of the machine" by writers from Milton to William Morris. "I do not claim that they represent truth," wrote Jennings in his introduction, "they are too varied, even contradictory, for that. But they represent human experience. They are the record of mental events. Events of the heart" (Jennings, Jennings, and Madge 2012: 19). Jennings soon became "the biggest single inspiration" to *Isles of Wonder*: "Its most striking images—an industrial powerhouse rising before your eyes, a green hill disgorging workers into the arena, rings forged in molten steel—all come from here" (Boyce 2012: 13–14).

Boyle drew inspiration not only from Jennings's *Pandaemonium*, but from Jennings's films as well. Philip C. Logan's comments on Jennings's wartime documentaries are no less applicable to the style of *Isles of Wonder*:

the audience is presented with almost painterly impressionistic images of chimneys, housing and industry, which often dwarf the inhabitants. Space and place, landscape and environment contextualise and locate spare time activity. Out of the consequences of industrialism comes a creative form of popular expression, with its own strangeness and beauty. (2011: 110)

No less striking are the similarities between Boyle's and Jennings's use of pop music. Keith Beattie records how, during the shooting of *Heart of Britain*, the Coventry Blitz of November 1940 shifted the focus of Jennings's film:

the reworked film that stemmed from the raid on Coventry also incorporated an increased use of music, with the effect that music becomes, together with the focus on Coventry, a central structuring device ... music—and references in the commentary to music and singing, and the partial displacement of commentary by music—serves as a theme or notation, running throughout the film. (2010: 51)

Comparably, *Isles of Wonder* nearly eliminated dialogue in favor of music, song, and film clips.

Jennings's *Pandaemonium* also provides the strongest point of comparison between *Isles of Wonder* and the stage adaptation of *Frankenstein*. On stage, Frankenstein's Creature encounters an enormous machine throwing off sparks and that resembles a steam locomotive fitted with huge gears. The machine is visually evocative of the machinery that marks the coming of the Industrial Revolution during the "Pandemonium" sequence in *Isles of Wonder*; both were designed by Mark Tildesley.[7]

Sensory Overload

Isles of Wonder is structured around live-action segments in the stadium alternating with short, pre-recorded original films (as distinct from the many clips from feature films used in the stadium). These original shorts, shown on huge screens in the stadium and broadcast in the television feeds, allowed Team Boyle to reset the playing areas in the stadium multiple times to accommodate the five live-action episodes: "Green and Pleasant Land," "Pandaemonium," "Second to the Right, and Straight on till Morning" (hereafter the NHS segment), "Frankie and June Say, Thanks Tim" (hereafter "Thanks Tim"), and "Abide with Me." Interspersed with the episodes of film and live-action performance, the mandated elements of the Olympic protocols were treated with imagination and humor.

The first of these original shorts, played during the countdown, is a journey down the River Thames from its source in Kemble that is anything but a leisurely travelogue. Opening with two young boys playing near a rivulet of water, the film moves across England, following the Thames from its headwaters through London to the new Olympic Stadium. Meanwhile, huge blue cloths pour over the stadium audience as they are baptized into the ceremony to mark the beginning of *Isles of Wonder*. The Thames journey film is shot at a dizzying pace, covering the ninety miles in about three minutes. This opening film sets out the many ways in which *Isles of Wonders* celebrates Britain's beauty, London's intensely urban environment and a population thrilled to have the Olympic Games. When the film reaches the stadium, the fast-motion photography and editing tempo accelerate even faster as it zooms through tube tunnels to images of the first iterations of London's Underground. Likewise, Boyle uses very brief clips of British champions from earlier Olympic Games as well as program covers from the 1908 London Games and archival footage of the young Elizabeth at the 1948 London Games. From this early point, chronology is shattered. The past is made to point to and celebrate the present moment.

Once the camera reaches the Olympic Stadium, it discovers an idyllic scene of a very different Britain: William Blake's "Green and Pleasant Land," which has served as a prologue for the stadium audience. Here is an agrarian, pre-industrial culture at leisure: Men play football; women toss apples; children frolic in a maypole dance; live sheep cavort on the meadow (Figure 7). It is a world at harmony with nature that is about to be transformed before our eyes.

At one end of the stadium stands a terraced hill topped by an enormous oak tree, identified by some as the Glastonbury Tor. The arrival of a horse-drawn coach carrying the civil engineer Isambard Kingdom Brunel (1806–59) marks the beginning of the second live-action episode, "Pandemonium." Brunel, played by Kenneth Branagh, delivers Caliban's "Be not afeard" speech from *The Tempest*, the only words of dialogue heard in *Isles of Wonder* that are neither sung live nor sampled from a recorded song or film. For the next seventeen minutes, Dame

Figure 7 *The "Green and Pleasant Land" episode in* Isles of Wonder. *Photo by Ben Stansall/AFP/Getty Images.*

Evelyn Glennie leads 1,000 volunteer drummers in performing Underworld's "And I Will Kiss" as the immense oak tree on the Tor unbelievably rises up. From beneath it, thousands of workers emerge: a population that will create the Industrial Revolution and London's urban environment.[8]

"Pandemonium" foregrounds the genius of British engineering in the nineteenth century. Top-hatted men, described by many as industrialists, mime the shoveling of coal as the technologies of the Industrial Revolution appear (Figure 8). Groups as disparate as the Grimethrope Colliery Band, pearly kings and queens, Sergeant Pepper's Lonely Hearts Club, Chelsea pensioners, and the *Windrush* Caribbean immigrants underscore that modern, multicultural London has been forged by diverse races and classes. A group of suffragettes enacts Emily Wilding Davison's death after she ventured on to the racetrack and was struck by King George V's horse at the Epsom Derby in 1913. In the midst of the thunderous drumming and frenzied action, the drumming and music subside to a soft whistling as everyone on the pitch pauses to remember those who died in the First World War. From near the Tor, a river of glowing molten iron flows into a huge ring. Once complete, the ring rises up to join four others that together form the Olympic Rings, which rain down fireworks to conclude "Pandemonium."

The title of this episode also describes its *mise en scène*: chaotic, turbulent, confusing. Like many pageants, "Pandemonium" creates sensory overload. The visual spectacle sees seven enormous chimneys (actually inflatables) rise from the stadium floor while its grassy coverings are removed to reveal an urban pavement that resembles the aerial view of London familiar in the title sequence of BBC soap opera *EastEnders*. Its sense of time is elastic. Rather than depicting London's past as a linear chronology, it is seen as a panorama of simultaneity. The cadence of 1,000 drummers creates a sense of urgency and unstoppable momentum. As well as the visual

Figure 8 *The "Pandemonium" episode in* Isles of Wonder. *Photo by Quinn Rooney/Getty Images.*

spectacle and thunderous drumming, Boyle further engaged the spectators' senses by using the actual smell of cordite in the stadium during this sequence.

One of the unavoidable questions was how the Queen would travel to the opening ceremony. Played while the stadium floor was dark, the six-minute film "Happy and Glorious" reimagines the royal progress as James Bond (played by Daniel Craig) arrives at Buckingham Palace to escort the Queen to the Olympic Stadium. Together they seem to enter a helicopter whose travel across London offers a second montage of aerial shots: crowds salute them; Churchill's statue comes alive; London's support for the Queen, James Bond, and the Games is palpable. With impeccable timing, the film ends as a real (live-action) helicopter arrives and hovers over the stadium. From it, two figures jump: one wearing a pink dress and another in suit and tie glide down under ram-air parachutes emblazoned with the Union Jack as the nine notes of Monty Norman's iconic fanfare from the James Bond theme boom out. The next moment, the stadium announcer introduces, "Her Majesty, Queen Elizabeth and the President of the IOC, Jacques Rogge"; she calmly walks to her seat wearing the pink dress that the audience last saw parachuting from the helicopter. The Queen's agreement to appear in the film suggests that royal protocols were less rigid and informed by much better sense of humor than those of the IOC. The "Happy and Glorious" sequence is not only a technical triumph, but also a wry riff on the mandated Olympic protocols.

In that brief interval occupied by the film, the stadium floor has been again transformed for the third live-action sequence "Second to the Right, and Straight on till Morning," which celebrates the National Health Service (NHS) and British children's literature. With the stadium now largely dark and Mike Oldfield performing his "Tubular Bells," nurses dressed in striped uniforms, aprons, and old-fashioned caps wheel in scores of children in hospital beds, many of which are actually trampolines, covered in illuminated sheets. They are choreographed to form the logo for the Great Ormond

Street Hospital, spell out the children's hospital informal name "GOSH" and then the huge letters "NHS." The program as well as stadium announcer locate the NHS as the fulfillment of Aneurin Bevan's belief that "no society can call itself civilized if a sick person is denied medical aid because of a lack of means" (qtd. in Boyle 2012b). The children are not quite ready for sleep. As J. K. Rowling reads from J. M. Barrie's *Peter Pan*, the children's night-time fears come to life in the great villains of British children's literature.[9] Order will be restored by thirty-two Mary Poppins nannies who fly into the stadium, their umbrellas acting as parachutes (Figure 9). To the strains of "In Dulce Jubilo," the children have a last dance and settle in their beds for sleep.

A second question that loomed over the opening ceremony was how *Chariots of Fire*, Hugh Hudson's Oscar-winning film about Britain's runners at the 1924 Olympic Games, would figure in the opening ceremony. Its instantly recognizable musical score by the Greek-British Vangelis had topped the

Figure 9 *Seen against a sea of LED pixels, multiple Mary Poppins fly into the stadium during "Second to the Right, and Straight on till Morning" (NHS segment) of* Isles of Wonder. *Photo by Morgan Treacy/INPHO via Getty Images.*

Billboard 200 charts in 1981 and stayed on the British charts
until 1983. Leading up to the 2012 Games, the film and its
score were focal points in television ads, the UK torch relay,
and the rerelease of the remastered film. A stage adaptation
of the film by Mike Bartlett opened at the Hampstead Theatre
in May 2012 and transferred to the West End, where it ran
until January 2013. By July 2012, Britain, if not the world,
was saturated with various iterations of *Chariots of Fire*. Boyle
again turned to humor. As Simon Rattle conducts the London
Symphony Orchestra, a spotlight picks out the performer
who plays a single note, a D, thousands of times. It is Rowan
Atkinson as Mr. Bean, made famous on British television in the
1990s. The music may be stirring and inspirational, but Mr.
Bean is bored by the monotony of playing a single note. He
looks at his watch; he checks his phone; he sneezes and then
drifts off to a fantasy in which he is running on the beach at
St. Andrews in the most famous sequence in *Chariots of Fire*.
In vintage Mr. Bean style, he finds a way to "win" the race
that involves his signature underhanded, silent-film physical
comedy.

Boyle here inserts another of the Olympic mandated
protocols as the flag is raised and anthems played. For a
third time, the entire pitch is cleared for the final live-action
sequence, "Thanks Tim." Two houses occupy the stadium
floor: one is a realistic family house, meant to suggest a typical
contemporary dwelling, populated by an extended mixed-race
family; the other is an oversized, cartoonish projection house.
Pre-recorded film of the family watching television together is
intercut with live-action as very brief clips, many under three
seconds, from British soap operas, sitcoms, and a memorable
Michael Fish BBC weather forecast appear on the stadium
screens and on the projection house (Figure 10). The teenaged
June emerges from the family house with her sister for a night
out. Their Tube travel is cleverly simulated by dozens of curved
fluorescent tubes carried overhead by dancers to suggest
various Underground lines known by their colors. June and
Frankie briefly glimpse each other in a moment that directly

recalls the love at first sight in *Romeo and Juliet*; a memorable clip from Baz Luhrmann's 1996 film makes the comparison explicit. By now, hundreds of young dancers fill the stadium floor choreographed in various formations, including the peace symbol (another British invention). Frankie finds the phone June has lost and in lieu of spoken dialogue, they exchange text messages that are displayed on the stadium's various screens. When Frankie tracks down June to return her phone, the need for dialogue is obviated when he introduces himself by opening his jacket to reveal a Katharine Hamnett oversized white message T-shirt: "Frankie Say Relax." Their "big kiss" is intercut with comparable moments from movies (including *A Matter of Life and Death*, Powell and Pressburger, 1946) and life (Prince William and Kate Middleton) and followed by a live performance of "Bonkers" by Dizzee Rascal. The sequence concludes as the family house rises up to reveal Tim Berners-Lee, inventor of the World Wide Web. The pageant's motto,

Figure 10 *The motto of the pageant displayed in the "Thanks Tim" segment in* Isles of Wonder. *The illuminated projection house seen at center. Photo by Jason Florio/Corbis via Getty Images.*

"This is for Everyone," is displayed on the LED pixel panels across the entire stadium.

The sound montage includes dialogue from dozens of films and scores of British pop songs. Sometimes the songs and film soundtracks overlap as when the soundtrack from the film *Kes* (Loach, 1969) plays over the Beatles' "She Loves You." Many of these may be meaningless outside of Britain, but were very familiar to British audiences. The overwhelming impression is not of thousands of performers doing exactly the same thing at exactly the same moment, but of thousands of people enjoying their leisure by dancing in their own style. Whereas Beijing featured mass choreography, astonishing because so many performers moved with such precision in lockstep with each other, Boyle's pageant shows people moving—working, traveling, dancing, and marching—not as one, but as many. All five of the live-action pageant episodes can be read in dialogue with the 2008 opening ceremony. In London, performers retain a modicum of agency and individuality, all moving together but as individuals.

A fourth short film shows clips from the 1948 Olympic Games and footage of the Olympic torch's journey across the UK and to the stadium in a speedboat by David Beckham and Jade Bailey. Like earlier films in the pageant, this one again moves across London—now at night and again to underscore the public's ecstatic welcome. The announcer calls for a moment of silence to "respect our memorial wall for friends and family who cannot be here tonight," as dozens of photos of absent friends materialize on screens.

With the stadium floor again cleared and glowing a flame orange, *Isles of Wonder* segues into performance of "Mortality," a ballet choreographed and performed by Akram Khan with a company of professional dancers. The ballet features a boy, a much younger version of the principal dancer, who reminds his older self of the inevitability of aging and death. Against the pulse of a throbbing heartbeat (similarly heard at the beginning of the stage production of *Frankenstein*), Emeli Sandé sings the hymn "Abide with Me."

After the parade of athletes, the stadium again is plunged into darkness and the Arctic Monkeys perform "Come Together" as hundreds of bicycle riders outfitted with enormous illuminated wings to represent doves of peace circle the outer track. One rises up to fly the length of the stadium, its wings gracefully flapping. After speeches by Coe and Rogge, the Queen recites her designed line to open the Games, the Olympic flag is carried into the stadium and hoisted. While the oaths are taken by athletes, judges, and coaches, the speedboat arrives at the stadium with the torch, which is carried into the stadium by the British rower and five-time Olympic champion Steve Redgrave. The center of the stadium floor is covered by the 204 huge copper petals, one for each of the participating nations, arrayed on long stems to form an enormous flower head. After they are lighted, the stems rise up to form the Olympic cauldron designed by Thomas Heatherwick. In and outside the stadium, fireworks explode as clips of great Olympic victories play. In the final segment of *Isles of Wonder*, Paul McCartney sings a few bars of "And in The End" and "Hey Jude" concludes nearly four hours of dancing, drumming, LED display, film and television clips, music, pyrotechnics, and historical reimagining.

Site-specificity

An estimated 70,000 volunteers were needed for the London Olympic Games. An astonishing 240,000 came forward. Eisya Sofia Azman surveyed the volunteers to discover a wide range of motivations, but concluded that involvement with sports, the desire "to give something back to the Games" and "to ensure the successful delivery of the 2012 Games" (2014: 42) dominated. Almost all of the volunteers performing in the NHS segment were staff members of the NHS. The names of all the volunteers who contributed to *Isles of Wonder* were printed in the program for the opening ceremony.

The many referents, clips, extracts, allusions, and tributes
in *Isles of Wonder* weave a rich texture that redefines British
heritage and cultural literacy. Most of the musical excerpts
might have been lost on many people over the age of fifty. At one
level, a global audience enjoyed a riotous spectacle of sight and
sound featuring international pop stars like David Bowie, Paul
McCartney, and Mick Jagger. Some elements of the pageant,
familiar hymns like "Jerusalem" and "Abide with Me," found
strong emotional resonances with British viewers, especially the
latter hymn, which has been performed before the FA Cup Final
and the Rugby League Challenge Cup since the 1920s. British
audiences were more likely to recognize the films (almost all of
which were British) seen in clips; many of these films did not
find commercial distribution out of the UK. An audible "awww"
could be heard from the stadium audience in response to one of
the longer film clips played: a full six seconds from *Gregory's
Girl* (Forsyth, 1981). Older viewers and film buffs might have
appreciated that the Frankie and June take their names from the
protagonists in *A Matter of Life and Death*.

The Olympic Games are awarded to a city, but Boyle's
pageant is site-specific to the UK, to London, and to the
boroughs of East London. These three locales are nested
almost like Russian dolls, so that UK viewers were privileged
over international audiences; even more privileged were
Londoners, with East London enjoying the greatest privilege.
Isles of Wonder embeds Northern Ireland, Scotland, Wales,
and England (the "four nations" that make up the UK)
in many ways. Four children's choirs sing iconic songs in
iconic places; "Danny Boy," for instance, is performed on the
Giant's Causeway in Northern Ireland. Each of these choral
performances contains a brief clip of a moment of sporting
glory. Past heroes from non-Olympic sports that are extremely
popular in and native to the UK, such as football, rugby, and
cricket, feature alongside former UK Olympians.

Greater London is crossed three times in the filmed content
screened in *Isles of Wonder*: first in tracing the course of the
River Thames; then when the helicopter carries the Queen

and James Bond to the stadium; finally, the journey of the Olympic torch sees a brilliantly illuminated city of bridges and landmarks. Both of the previous Games held in London appear in footage, posters, and memorabilia. Images of great British engineering achievements, especially those that might be associated with Brunel, figure prominently.

Boyle takes considerable care to celebrate the people and culture of the five boroughs of East London—Hackney, Greenwich, Newham, Tower Hamlets, and Waltham Forest— that were targeted for renewal in the Olympic Games planning documents.[10] Zimbalist writes, "Although they each have their distinctive traits, as a group they are characterized by rising population numbers, a relatively young and minority demographic, and comparatively high levels of social deprivation (measured by levels of employment, income, health, skills, education, housing, and crime, and certain attributes of the living environment)" (2015: 107). Beckham, originally from Leytonstone in Waltham Forest, is at the helm of the speedboat that brings Jade Bailey, who represents not only British (non-Olympic) football but also Waltham Forest, carrying the Olympic torch to the stadium. The Stratford station can be glimpsed in the lightning montage of tube travel. The 3 Mills studio in Stratford hosted rehearsals of *Isles of Wonder*. Children from "local schools in the six boroughs" (Boyle 2012b: "DVD Commentary") were recruited as performers. Boyle describes the East End as home for many immigrants, including some who traveled on the *Windrush*. Dizzee Rascal, from Tower Hamlets, wears a cap with the initials "LDN" and a club jacket displaying the "E3" postal code.

The narratives of the live-action pageant episodes were accessible, but always richly encoded. Perhaps this is most clearly seen in the instance of Berners-Lee. When the family house rose up to reveal a man at a computer, NBC commentators expressed befuddlement and invited their American audience viewers to google Sir Tim Berners-Lee. "If you haven't heard of him," said NBC's Meredith Viera, "we haven't either" (qtd. in Wagg 2015: 25).

Technologies

There are many versions of *Isles of Wonder* in circulation. No single real-time version includes all the images produced or all film clips that were used in the four-hour spectacular. During the third live-action sequence, "Thanks Tim," images and film clips appeared on all four sides as well as the roof of the projection house. Often several images were projected simultaneously. The "Extras" segment in the BBC/IBC five-DVD set contain many but not all of these. Some of these images, of Ken Livingstone, for instance, appear only very, very briefly.

Each seat in the stadium had a nine-LED display panel (the "pixels") from which a "video landscape" created visuals such as silhouetted fuchsia dancers or the British Union Jack flowing across the stadium audience. The pixel displays "mapped to the space inhabited by the entire [stadium] audience. ... over 70,500 pixel tablets were produced for each seat [*sic*] in the stadium, and video emerged from its two-dimensional world to become 3D; the audience members integrated into the show itself ... by creating the world's largest video screen to date."[11] These patterns immersed the audience in constantly changing colors and patterns, only glimpsed in many of the video recordings, but perfectly consonant with the propensity of pageants to dissolve the boundaries between performer and spectator.

Isles of Wonder bombards its audience with immense amounts of information. The pace of the live-action episodes builds from the leisurely pastimes of pre-industrial Britain to the furious pace of the flash cuts in "Thanks Tim." Only the brief, subdued commemoration of the First World War and the "Abide with Me"/memorial wall sequence step away from the frenetic pace that otherwise dominates *Isles of Wonder* from the moment of Brunel's arrival. Each of the shards and fragments of British film, children's literature, music and television contributes to a composite quite unlike previous iterations of British heritage.

If the Beijing games focused on paper, movable type, the compass, and gunpowder as China's contributions to world civilization, *Isles of Wonder* argues for Britain's children's literature, the NHS, the Industrial Revolution, music and film, the World Wide Web, and a "bonkers" sense of humor. In his commentary to the BBC broadcast, Boyle talks about how *Isles of Wonder* embraces low culture: "I've always been a believer in trash culture and it becomes high culture" (2012b: DVD commentary). The utopian vision of *Isles of Wonder* is one in which the pleasures of a night out connect people, more specifically, the young, mixed-race Frankie and June. What binds Britain and much of the world together is the shared cultural literacy that instantly recognizes the opening bars of "(I Can't Get No) Satisfaction" and the image of Mick Jagger as he appeared forty-seven years earlier.

Boyle begins his program notes for *Isles of Wonder* with the observation, "At some point, most nations experience a revolution that changes everything about them. The United Kingdom had a revolution that changed the whole of human existence" (Boyle 2012a: 11). He concludes his brief note,

But we hope that through all the noise and excitement you'll glimpse a single golden thread of purpose—the idea of Jerusalem—of a better world, the world of real freedom and true equality, a world that can be built through the prosperity of industry, through the caring nation that built the welfare state, through the joyous energy of popular culture through the dream of universal communication. A belief that we can build Jerusalem. And that it will be for everyone. (11)

Isles of Wonder recasts British heritage in profound ways. With the exception of the *Windrush* passengers, gone is any whiff of, let alone nostalgia for, the British Empire. What is taken from Milton and Shakespeare is wrenched from its original context and reimagined. Caliban's lines, after all, are addressed to Stephano and Trinculo as they plot to murder

Prospero and usurp his power. Milton's pandemonium is the
capital of hell and the seat of Satan's evil. Here, however,
Shakespeare and Milton are made to speak to a tumultuous
British past that made the present possible. Britain is great
because in building bridges, tunnels, and the World Wide Web,
its engineers used technology to better the lives of ordinary
people. Both Boyce and Boyle imagine nineteenth-century
British engineering as altruistic. For Boyce, "Maybe the most
important lesson of [*Pandaemonium, 1660–1886*] is how
clearly it demonstrates that although the Industrial Revolution
brought unprecedented wealth, it was not created by people
who were interested in money" (2012: 17). Similarly, Boyle
describes Brunel and Berners-Lee as "famous figures who
insisted on their work being publicly owned" (2013: 406). The
highly selective treatment of history that is characteristic of
pageants is perhaps most evident in *Isles of Wonder* in regard
to this view of nineteenth-century industrialists. The present
that British engineering created is indeed wonderful, not least
because it connects people: by phones and the World Wide
Web, by the shared experience of television, film, and music
and by a new literacy. There is a circularity in the pageant:
it began with a green and pleasant land that afforded people
leisure and pleasure and returns to celebrate the leisure and
pleasure found by two very young kids who have their own
cellphones (and access to the World Wide Web), independence,
and a weekend night out. The children's choirs, the teenaged
Frankie, June, and their many friends, the young patients at
the Great Ormond Street Hospital, and the celebration of
British children's literature all project images of Britain as a
very young country.

Response

The twenty-first century is open season on mega-events like the
opening ceremonies. MacAloon recalled that "what made the

Crystal Palace [1851] so powerful a symbol and so provocative an event in Victorian cultural history was its calling forth of commentary, celebration, and criticism from every quarter and current of British social opinion" (2008: 130). Commentary and criticism were certainly much easier to broadcast in 2012 than in 1851. Nonetheless, several commentators document the largely positive response to *Isles of Wonder* on social media and in the British daily press (see Bryant 2015; Wagg 2015). Among the negative responses, MP Aidan Burley, for instance, tweeted that the opening ceremony was "leftie multi-cultural crap."[12] Perhaps the most damning criticism came from Peter Hitchens in *The Mail on Sunday* who saw *Isles of Wonder* as the dawning "of a new age in which our proud past is ridiculed and our history rewritten" (Hitchens 2012). Despite Hitchens's lament, the political dimension of *Isles of Wonder* sought and in large measure found uncontroversial praise. Steve Richards (2012), writing in the *Independent*, summed up what would be obvious to any Briton, but might have been missed by many others:

As the NHS was celebrated vividly with bright lights and hundreds of dancing nurses, I was reminded of Hamlet, the scene when Hamlet asks the players to act out his father's murder. The murderer Claudius is in the audience when the play is subsequently performed. At the opening ceremony, David Cameron must have felt a little like Claudius as he watched Danny Boyle's players: A Prime Minister who seeks to overhaul the NHS with contentious reforms, watching a jubilant portrayal of the NHS as it is and was. Danny Boyle was the mischievous Hamlet. The players performed. Cameron was the uneasy ruler. Boyle knew what he was doing, just as Hamlet did.

In the *Guardian*, Mark Lawson praised the ceremony as "a triumph of agitprop theatre" (qtd. in Boyle 2013: 410). As skeptical as many centrist and right-wing publications were of Boyce's background as a columnist for *Living Marxism*, a reminder of which appeared in every episode of *Coronation Street* that he scripted, their immediate response in Britain was positive. Boyle, however, attributes the positive reception of *Isles of Wonder* to its ability to move "beyond politics": "People asked how the opening ceremony could please so many people, but the values it believed in are those that we hold true despite our politics: tolerance, dissent, inclusivity, engineering, culture, humour, ambition, modesty" (2013: 411).

The response from academics has been less enthusiastic about the opening ceremony. Christopher Bryant, for instance, writes that "Britain abroad in the empire is absent" (340) and ludicrously rebukes Boyle for "allow[ing] no hint that there was a referendum pending on Scottish independence" (2015: 341). Stephen Wagg's (2015: 46) otherwise excellent article on *Isles of Wonder* laments what he finds lacking, including imperialism, City of London bankers, the Second World War, the 2003 invasion of Iraq, and Margaret Thatcher, all of which belong in a history textbook, but hardly in a utopian pageant. More in line with Lawson's view of the pageant as agit-prop, Anita Biressi and Heather Nunn suggested that "*Isles of Wonder* arguably offered a counter-history and a counter-argument; one which reminded British audiences as *citizens* and social actors why the public sector (the supported arts, welfare, health and perhaps even public service television) should be valued and defended and why social enfranchisement mattered" (2013: 117).

Conclusion

The three pageants used as exemplars here cross six centuries (from *c.*1470 to 1909–12 and 2012) and very different cultures, but like all pageants, these three are deeply wedded to their particular time and place. Their audiences—medieval English Catholics, women's suffrage supporters or possible converts to the cause, anyone with access to a television in 2012—could hardly be more diverse. The great men of history dominate many pageants, but these three somewhat unusually afford equity to or emphasis on women. The three pageants also indicate the very broad range of pageant venues—the streets of medieval York, purpose-built English halls and theatres, and a state-of-the-art 80,000-seat stadium—that demand a very wide range of dramaturgical tactics, owing in part to the number of performers, most of whom were amateurs. The Noah pageants cast fewer than a dozen people performing in a relatively restricted playing area of (and near) the pageant wagon. Performed by scores of women (and one man), *A Pageant of Great Women* was played indoors in halls and theatres that typically accommodated between 500 and 1,500. The 7,500 performers in *Isles of Wonder* filled more than 7,000 square meters or nearly two acres of the stadium pitch. All three drew on the skills of professionals. The Noah pageants may not have had professional actors, but the ark was designed by shipwrights.

Despite profound differences, these three pageants illustrate the most persistent features of the idiom. Each pageant aspired to create a spectacle that imparted an aspiration: salvation, enfranchisement, inclusivity. The Noah pageant was only one episode in the medieval cycles, which could occupy twenty hours of a single day or be spread out over several days. *Isles of Wonder* fulfilled expectations as a spectacular extravaganza that encapsulated a version of British history, an accomplishment that many welcomed and enjoyed. As a counter-hegemonic pageant, *A Pageant of Great Women* was produced with more limited resources, but reached wide audiences in and outside the metropolitan centers of London and Liverpool.

All three, like most, pageants look to past events and compress decades, centuries, even millennia into minutes or hours of stage time. That often-extreme compression of time creates a permeable boundary between past and present, the distant and the immediate, perhaps even the sacred and the mundane. Common to pageants, and sometimes corollary to the compression of time, is the dissolution of the barriers between performer and spectator through physical proximity, communal singing or movement, and digital technologies in pursuit of *communitas*. Pageants very commonly seek that organic sense of individuals united by shared beliefs, which are often narratively constructed as an ideal, a utopian vision: the community of Christ, equality for women, the Olympic ideals.

In projecting a utopian vision by staging the past in a familiar, often site-specific, location, pageants invite the audience to engage with physical realities rather than with remote abstractions or distant tales. Audiences value the bodily presence of the numerous pageant performers over the simulation, however spectacular or sophisticated, that might be achieved using projection techniques, CGI, or other technologies. At some level, the audience recognizes the humanity it shares with the many performers.

While pageant history lacks the continuous traditions that link the tragedies of Sophocles, Shakespeare, and Miller, several theatrical tactics and strategies mark pageants as a distinct theatrical idiom: site-specificity, presentational style, personation, audience performativity, encoded vernacular forms, inventive technologies, historical episodes, elaborate costuming, mass choreography, the manipulation of both time and space, extensive use of song and music, and wide, if not populist, appeal. Although not every pageant displays each of these features and what each of these means varies greatly over time, these characteristics suggest a pageant's dissimilarity with much of mainstream theatre and affinities with other theatrical idioms such as processions, circuses, masques, and opera.

Pageants are very closely related to a variety of other counter-hegemonic theatrical or paratheatrical forms, such as street protests, marches, demonstrations, *grèves*, and riots that aim to create public spectacles through personation but lack the narrative thread that might make them pageants. Similarly, there now exists a growing number of mass gatherings, what Roche and others call "mega-events," that attract international audiences, extensive press coverage, and sometimes notoriety. When Richard Wagner founded an opera festival in a Bavarian town in 1876, the leisure and mobility of potential audiences were essential factors to the success of his project. As leisure time, disposable income, and mobility increased, tourism became a significant industry not just in Bayreuth or Western Europe, but globally. Destinations such as Pamplona, Sturgis, Lourdes, and Glastonbury are nearly synonymous with the mass gatherings they host, which have redefined the economy if not the identity of these places. The days and even weeks preceding sporting competitions like the Super Bowl or the World Cup Final have become mega-events in themselves. Some of these, like Mardi Gras and Burning Man, aggressively pursue an escape from the constraints of modern urban life; many integrate pageants as they invent their own traditions. These and other pageants spring from tourist initiatives. In the twenty-first century, the audience for many pageants is not a local, native population eager to celebrate its heritage, but instead tourists in search of an "authentic" cultural experience. For more than sixty years, Ireland required transatlantic passengers to "stopover" in Shannon airport in order to spur economic development in the west of Ireland. Bryan MacMahon's *Pageant of Ireland* was staged as dinner theatre in a nearby castle for a ready-made audience of transatlantic travelers waiting for their morning flight home. It ran for fifteen years.

The best-funded, most elaborate pageants in the early twenty-first century, the opening ceremonies of the Olympic Games, continue to celebrate a place and now carry the clear expectation of an innovative spectacle celebrating the host nation's identity and contributions to world culture with strong emphasis on the progressive Olympic values, particularly inclusiveness, environmental awareness, and gender equity. Because opening ceremonies are recorded and can be easily accessed online, increasingly visible lines of continuity and discontinuity allow the pageants to be read in dialogue with each other. And, perhaps not unlike the medieval guilds who must have seen their pageants in competitions with those of other guilds, any future opening ceremony will be judged in comparison to those in Beijing and London.

Despite the glut of entertainment choices in the twenty-first century, the performative impulse remains undiminished in our age. In fact, the many channels of social media invite individuals to blend the ludic and the participatory by digitally engaging with a community that exists only in a cyber world. Video-gaming's use of avatars, itself a form of personation, allows individuals to step outside an identity they may find static, confining, or unfulfilling. Pageants have long offered such ludic opportunities and will long continue to do so.

NOTES

Introduction

1   See https://www.nyhistory.org/web/crossroads/gallery/celebrations/federal_ship_hamilton.html.

2   See Corney (2004: 73–82).

3   "Louis N. Parker, The Man Who Wrote 'Pomander Walk'," *New York Times Sunday Magazine*: 6.

4   *Belfast Newsletter*, July 12, 1888: 8.

5   [London] *Times*, August 19, 1896: 8.

6   In his "Preface" to *To-morrow*, MacKaye writes: "Positive eugenics is concerned with the improvement of the human breed, through selection; negative eugenics—with its safeguarding from racial poisons, through the spread of medical knowledge. Both aspects are, of course, incalculably important" (vi).

7   *Bulletin of the American Pageant Association*, July 15, 1914, 5: 2.

8   Thomas Wood Stevens was Professor of Dramatic Arts at Carnegie Institute of Technology in Pittsburgh; George Pierce Baker was Professor of Dramatic Literature at Harvard University; Mary Porter Beegle was Director of Physical Education at Barnard College; Withington taught English at Indiana University and later Smith College; Peter W. Dykema was Professor of Music and Lecturer on Festivals at the University of Wisconsin. Even more members of the APA taught at smaller normal schools, which typically focused on teacher preparation, or at American high schools.

9   *A Manual of Pageantry* was published for the Indiana University Extension Service. Extension services bring academic expertise, typically in the agricultural sciences or education, to the community.

10 The Redress of the Past: Historical Pageants in Britain project
    website: https://historicalpageants.ac.uk/.

11 Wallis describes the Liverpool civic weeks in the 1920s as a
    "major ruse" (1995: 23).

12 *We Will Never Die*, radio broadcast recording, Ben Hecht
    Papers, Series 11: 1–4, Newberry Library, Chicago.

13 Grant Application to Gulbenkian Trust, T7, MA/NUIG.

Chapter 1

1 The exception is the Chester cycle, which employed Latin more
   freely. See Mills (2008: 138).

2 Duffy describes these Palm Sunday processions as the only
   other time in the liturgical year when the Eucharist was
   brought outside the church and then only in a procession
   around the church.

3 No line numbers in text.

4 Quotations in the text refer to the following online editions of
   the Noah pageants:

   • Chester, "Noah's Flood": https://medievalit.com/home/
     edrama/chester-plays/noahs-flood/

   • N-Town, "Noah and the Flood": https://medievalit.com/
     home/edrama/n-town/play-4-noahs-flood/

   • York, Play 8: https://quod.lib.umich.edu/c/cme/York/1:9?rgn
     =div1;view=fulltext

   • York, Play 9: https://quod.lib.umich.edu/c/cme/York/1:10?rg
     n=div1;view=fulltext

   • Towneley, "The Play of Noah": http://sites.fas.harvard.
     edu/~chaucer/special/litsubs/drama/noah.html

   • Newcastle, "Noah and Lamech": https://books.google.com/
     books?id=ubyn-MqC2CgC&pg=PR8&dq=pre-shakespearea
     n+specimens&hl=en&newbks=1&newbks_redir=0&sa=X&
     ved=2ahUKEwioqK6dieLqAhUWlXIEHTE1AaoQ6AEwAH
     oECAEQAg#v=onepage&q=Noah&f=false.

5 Wyatt (2013: 49–51) provides an overview of other Noah pageants, fragments, and records.

6 No lines assigned; between lines 160 and 161.

7 See "York Mystery Plays 2016: In the Wings," https://www.youtube.com/watch?v=sdlS-GFKN-k and "York Mystery Plays 2016: Behind the Scenes—Props," https://www.youtube.com/watch?v=YmhlxnI_-EQ).

8 See Davidson (1996): "the 'good hackestocke' (*chopping block*) noted by Shem's wife (III.69) is a kitchen item" (12).

9 See https://chestermysteryplays.com/resources/noahsflood2012.pdf.

Chapter 2

1 "The Purple, White & Green," *The Women's Exhibition 1909*, UDC Pamphlet Collection: Suffrage Pamphlets, PC/06/396-11/04, UDC Box 344, Women's Library at the London School of Economics (hereafter WL/LSE).

2 The women portrayed in this pictorial feature Mrs. Despard, b. 1844; Lady Henry Somerset, b. 1851; Anna Shaw, b. 1847; Mrs. Israel Zangwill, b. 1875/9; Hamilton, b. 1872; Frances Balfour, b. 1858; Beatrice Harraden, b. 1864; Mrs. Aryton, b. 1854; Mrs. Lyttleton, b. 1865; [Elizabeth] Garrett Anderson, b. 1836.

3 Membership in the AFL grew from 360 in 1910 to 550 in 1911 and 700 in 1912.

4 "Records of the Actresses' Franchise League," 2/AFL/C2, Box FL598, WL/LSE.

5 See Moran (2017).

6 See the Woman and Her Sphere website: https://womanandhersphere.com/tag/c-hedley-charlton/.

7 "Another Feminist Tempest over Matrimony," *Sunday Magazine*, October 3, 1909: 4.

8 In May 1918, the Aurora Overseas Auxiliary performed *The Temple of Fame: A Pageant of Famous Women*. In a small town, north of Toronto, Ontario, the pageant was focused

not on women's suffrage, as full voting equality was realized in the province of Ontario the year before, but rather, like Hamilton's pageant, on women's equality. The 1918 pageant drew on an earlier 1892 production originally performed in Hamilton, Ontario, and authored by J. Grant Henderson. The pageant was rewritten and revived in 2018 to commemorate the expansion of women's suffrage in Canada.

9   Three photographs of MacLachan's pageant are dated "1908–10" in the Women's Library ("Exhibitions, Fairs, Fêtes, Festivals: Women Through the Ages," Photograph Box E01, WL/LSE). The audience for MacLachan's pageant appears to be seated in bentwood chairs outside the hospital. Notations on one of the photographs identifies some characters in the pageant as Monica, mother of St. Augustine, Queen Margaret, and "Hermione, an ancient Egyptian," none of whom appear in any iteration of Hamilton's pageant. Moreover, MacLachan's pageant appears not to have included the three central characters in *A Pageant of Great Women*.

10 AFL Secretary's Report, Records of the Actresses' Franchise League, 2/AFL/A1/8, Box FL598, WL/LSE.

11 "The Storming of London," *The Vote*, November 18, 1909: 47.

12 WSPU letterhead in the Ellen Terry/Edith Craig Archive (hereafter ET/EC) archive suggests the pageant also was known as *Pageant of Brave Women* ("A Pageant of Great Women—Programmes," Box 13, Loan MS 125/7/4 Unbound, ET/EC).

13 "The Suffrage Shop," *The Vote*, June 11, 1910: 77.

14 "A Pageant of Great Women—Playscripts," Box 13, Loan MS 125/7/3 Unbound, ET/EC.

15 "Scala Theatre," [London] *Times*, November 13, 1909: 12.

16 "Conditions for Production of the Pageant of Great Women," Box 13, Loan MS 125/7/5 Unbound, ET/EC.

17 The rental of costumes was likely a source of income for Craig and her costume agency.

18 "Expenses and Arrangements for the production of THE [*sic*] PAGEANT OF GREAT WOMEN," Box 13, Loan MS 125/7/5 Unbound, ET/EC.

19 "Conditions for Production of the Pageant of Great Women," Box 13, Loan MS 125/7/5 Unbound, ET/EC. This document is

undated and unsigned, but it may have triggered the decision in New York to reject *A Pageant of Great Women* and instead to commission Augusta Kidder.

20   "Expenses and Arrangements for the production of THE [*sic*] PAGEANT OF GREAT WOMEN," Box 13, Loan MS 125/7/5 Unbound, ET/EC.

21   "Secretary's Report," Records of the Actresses' Franchise League, AFL/A/1a, WL/LSE: 2. The outbreak of the First World War entirely eclipsed the AFL's suffrage plays and entertainments. Under the auspices of the Women's Theatre Camps Entertainments, its energies were now trained on providing concerts and entertainments.

22   In *Ethel Smyth: A Biography*, St. John reports that Hamilton "was not Ethel's first choice. She had approached Masefield, Chesterton and Galsworthy without success" (1959: 151).

23   "Griselda Watkins, then a little under twenty-five, was his exact counterpart in petticoats; a piece of blank-minded young suburban young-womanhood caught into the militant suffrage movement and enjoying herself therein ... it was the policy of her particular branch of the suffrage movement to repress manifestations of masculine type in its members and encourage fluffiness of garb and appeal of manner. Griselda, who had a natural weakness for cheap finery, was a warm adherent of the policy, went out window-smashing in a picture-hat and cultivated ladylike charm" (Hamilton 1920: 20).

24   "Plays and Propaganda," *The Vote*, February 17, 1912: 200.

25   *The Vote*, February 10, 1912: 188 [no title].

26   "Costume Dinner and Pageant," *The Vote*, June 12, 1914: 121.

27   "American Suffrage Pageant," *New York Times*, March 12, 1911: 7.

28   "American Suffrage Play," *Sun* [New York], March 8, 1911: 9.

29   Curiously, the second copy required for the American copyright of *A Pageant of Great Women*, issued in Hamilton's name, was recorded in the Copyright Office in Washington, DC on March 11, 1911, the very day that the *New York Times* announced the decision against using her pageant.

30   Hewett points out that Columbia is often misidentified as Florence Fleming Noyes, who appeared as Liberty (2010: 71).

An extensive photographic record of the pageant and parade appears in Alan Taylor's "The 1913 Women's Suffrage Parade," *The Atlantic*, March 1, 2013, https://www.theatlantic.com/photo/2013/03/100-years-ago-the-1913-womens-suffrage-parade/100465/.

31 "The Pageant of the Idea," *New York Evening Post*, Saturday Supplement, May 10, 1913: 1.

32 Mary Porter Beegle's *Pageant of the Association of Working Women: The Romance of Work* appeared in same venue on May 15, 1914.

33 "Suffrage Pageant Seen by Hundreds," *Evening Star* [Washington], December 14, 1915: 9.

34 "Seneca Falls is Mecca for Woman's Party Leaders of Nation," *Auburn Citizen*, July 20, 1923: 6.

35 "Women and the Vote," *South Africa*, December 2, 1911: 475.

36 "Women Win Vote at May Revels," *Philadelphia Inquirer*, May 25, 1913: 2. Blair (1990: 39) reports that Mount Holyoke College in South Hadley, MA staged *A Pageant of Great Women* in 1912, but this may conflate Hamilton's pageant with the one held to mark the seventy-fifth anniversary of the school.

37 "Pageant of Great Women on View in Lansdowne," *Inquirer*, October 6, 1913: 2.

38 "'Without the Women Victory Will Tarry'," *Daily Graphic*, July 19, 1915: 1.

39 "Joan of Arc Day," [London] *Times*, April 23, 1917: 11.

Chapter 3

1 "Meet the IOC," No Boston Olympics website, https://www.nobostonolympics.org/meet_the_ioc.

2 "Curtis Proclaims the Olympics Open as 100,000 Look On," *New York Times*, July 31, 1932: S1.

3 See Trimborn (2008); Downing (2012).

4 The film was re-edited in 1955. To the point at which Hitler speaks, the soundtrack was exclusively instrumental. Riefenstahl's original editing, of course, may have been different. For details on the editing history of *Olympia*, see Downing (2012).

5 "China Celebrates Opening of Summer Olympics," NPR broadcast, August 8, 2008, https://www.npr.org/templates/story/story.php?storyId=93420251.

6 Reed denied that his song was about heroin use.

7 An excerpt of the steampunk scene from *Frankenstein* is available at https://www.youtube.com/watch?v=XKNNZKAu1 2g&list=PLJgBmjHpqgs4rKf-Xlvhbw2ihlM8eN4rT&index=7 &t=0s.

8 The program for *Isles of Wonder* specifically notes: "In 1709 Abraham Darby used coal to smelt iron in a small blast furnace in Coalbrookside. This is the beginning of the Industrial Revolution—an outburst of invention and innovation unparalleled in the history of the world" (Boyle 2012a: 16).

9 The British children's literature alluded to in *Isles of Wonder* includes J. M. Barrie's *Peter Pan*, Raymond Briggs's *The Snowman and the Snowdog*, Lewis Carroll's *Alice in Wonderland*, Ian Fleming's *Chitty Chitty Bang Bang*, Kenneth Grahame's *The Wind in the Willows*, J. K. Rowling's Harry Potter series, Dodie Smith's *One Hundred and One Dalmatians*, and P. L. Travers's *Mary Poppins*.

10 Some documents and reports include a sixth borough: Barking and Dagenham.

11 "LiveDesign Excellence Awards," LiveDesign website, June/July 2013, 22, https://www.livedesignonline.com/excellence-awards/london-2012-olympic-ceremonies.

12 "Aidan Burley Says 'Leftie Multi-cultural' Tweet Misunderstood," BBC News, July 28, 2012, https://www.bbc.com/news/uk-19025518.

BIBLIOGRAPHY

Ackroyd, Peter. (2011), *London Under*, London: Chatto & Windus.

Anderson, Benedict. (1983), *Imagined Communities: Reflections on the Origins and Spread of Nationalism*, London: Verso.

Anholt, Simon. (2007), *Competitive Identity: The New Brand Management for Nations, Cities and Regions*, Basingstoke: Palgrave Macmillan.

Arnold, David, Danny Boyle, Boyce F. Cottrell, Stephen Daldry, Es Devlin, Mark Fisher, and Kim Gavin. (2012), *London 2012 Olympic Games*, 5 DVDs, London: BBC Worldwide.

Auerbach, Erich. (1953), *Mimesis*, trans. Willard R. Trask, Princeton, NJ: Princeton University Press.

Auerbach, Nina. (1997), *Ellen Terry: Player in Her Time*, Philadelphia, PA: University of Pennsylvania Press.

Axelrod, Eric Peter. (2006), "Evacuation Day: New York City's Forgotten Past," *American History*, 43 (3): 28–35.

Azman, Eisya Sofia. (2014), "Understanding Motivations to Volunteer for the 2012 Summer Olympic and Paralympic Games," in Dikaia Chatziefstathiou and Norbert Müller (eds.), *Olympism, Olympic Education and Learning Legacies*, 40–9, Newcastle upon Tyne: Cambridge Scholars.

Barber, Lucy. (2004), *Marching on Washington: The Forging of an American Political Tradition*, Berkeley: University of California Press.

Barish, Jonas A. (1981), *Anti-theatrical Prejudice*, London: University of California Press.

Barmé, Geremie R. (2009), "China's Flat Earth: History and 8 August 2008," *China Quarterly*, 197: 64–86.

Barthes, Roland. (1972), *Critical Essays*, trans. Richard Howard, Evanston, IL: Northwestern University Press.

Bartlett, George B. and W. Gurney Benham. (1873), *Mrs. Jarley's Far-Famed Collection of Waxworks*, London: Samuel French.

Bates, Esther Willard. (1925), *The Art of Producing Pageants*, Boston: Walter H. Baker.

Bates, Esther Willard and William Orr. (1912), *Pageants and Pageantry*, New York: Ginn and Company.

Beadle, Richard. (1985), "The Shipwrights' Craft," in Paula Neuss (ed.), *Aspects of Early English Drama*, 50–61, Cambridge: D. S. Brewer.

Beadle, Richard. (2008), "The York Cycle," in Richard Beadle and Alan J. Fletcher (eds.), *The Cambridge Companion to Medieval English Theatre*, 99–124, Cambridge: Cambridge University Press.

Beadle, Richard. (2009), *York Mystery Plays: A Selection in Modern Spelling*, Oxford: Oxford University Press.

Beattie, Keith. (2010), *Humphrey Jennings*, Manchester: Manchester University Press.

Beckwith, Sarah. (2001), *Signifying God: Social Relation and Symbolic Act in the York Corpus Christi Plays*, Chicago: University of Chicago Press.

Beegle, Mary Porter and Jack Randall Crawford. (1916), *Community Drama and Pageantry*, New Haven, CT: Yale University Press.

Benjamin, Walter. (1979), *Reflections: Essays, Aphorisms, Autobiographical Writings*, New York: Harcourt Brace Jovanovich.

Benson, Edward Frederic (1934), *King Edward VII: An Appreciation*, London: Longmans.

Bergeron, David. (1971), *English Civic Pageantry 1558–1642*, Columbia: University of South Carolina Press.

Biressi, Anita and Heather Nunn. (2013), "The London 2012 Olympic Games Opening Ceremony: History Answers Back," *Journal of Popular Television*, 1 (1): 113–120.

Blair, Karen J. (1990), "Pageantry for Women's Rights: The Career of Hazel MacKaye, 1913–1923," *Theatre Survey*, 31 (1): 23–46.

Blodgett, Harriet. (1990), "Cicely Hamilton: Independent Feminist," *Frontiers: A Journal of Women Studies*, 11 (2/3): 99–104.

Blunt, Reginald. (1900), *An Illustrated Historical Handbook of the Parish of Chelsea*, London: The author.

Borsa, Mario. (1908), *The English Stage of To-Day*, London: John Lane.

Boyce, Frank Cottrell. (2012), "Foreword," in Humphrey Jennings, Mary-Lou Jennings, and Charles Madge, *Pandaemonium: 1660–1886: The Coming of the Machine as Seen by Contemporary Observers*, 13–15, London: Icon.

Boyle, Danny. (2012a), "Welcome to the Isles of Wonder," in *Isles of Wonder: London 2012 Olympic Games Opening Ceremony, 27 July 2012 – Îles Aux Merveilles: Cérémonie D'ouverture des Jeux Olympiques De Londres 2012, Le 27 Juillet 2012*, Teddington: Haymarket Network.

Boyle, Danny. (2012b), "DVD Commentary," *London 2012 Olympic Games*, 5 DVDs, London: BBC Worldwide.

Boyle, Danny and Brent Dunham. (2011), *Danny Boyle: Interviews*, Jackson: University Press of Mississippi.

Boyle, Danny in conversation with Amy Raphael. (2013), *Danny Boyle: Creating Wonder*, London: Faber & Faber.

Brown, John Russell. (1983), *The Complete Plays of the Wakefield Master*, London: Heinemann, 1983.

Browne, Elliot M. and Henzie Browne. (1981), *Two in One*, Cambridge: Cambridge University Press.

Browning, Mark. (2012), *Danny Boyle: Lust for Life*, London: Andrews.

Bryant, Chad Carl, Arthur Burns, and Paul Readman. (2016), *Walking Histories, 1800–1914*, London: Palgrave Macmillan.

Bryant, Christopher G. A. (2015), "National Art and Britain Made Real: The London 2012 Olympics Opening Ceremony," *National Identities*, 17 (3): 333–46.

Cameron, Rebecca. (2009), "From *Great Women* to *Top Girls*: Pageants of Sisterhood in British Feminist Theater," *Comparative Drama*, 43 (2): 143–66.

Carlson, Marvin A. (1989), *Places of Performance: The Semiotics of Theatre Architecture*, Ithaca, NY: Cornell University Press.

Carlson, Susan. (2000), "Comic Militancy: The Politics of Suffrage Drama," in Maggie B. Gale and Viv Gardner (eds.), *Women, Theatre and Performance: New Histories, New Historiographies*, 198–215, Manchester: Manchester University Press.

Carlson, Susan. (2001), "Portable Politics: Creating New Space for Suffrage-ing Women," *New Theatre Quarterly*, 17 (4): 334–46.

Carlson, Susan. (2013), "Suffrage Drama" in Mary Luckhurst (ed.), *A Companion to Modern British and Irish Drama, 1880–2005*, 99–109, Malden, MA: Blackwell.

Cawley, Arthur Clare, Marion Jones, Peter F. McDonald, and David Mills, eds. (1983), *The Revels History of Drama in English: Volume 1*, London: Methuen.

Chambers, Edmund Kerchever. (1903), *The Mediaeval Stage*, 2 vols, Oxford: Clarendon.

Cockin, Katharine. (1998), *Edith Craig (1869–1947)*, Dramatic
   Lives, London: Cassell.
Cockin, Katharine. (2005), "Cicely Hamilton's Warriors: Dramatic
   Reinventions of Militancy in the British Women's Suffrage
   Movement," *Women's History Review*, 14: 527–42.
Cockin, Katharine. (2017), *Edith Craig and the Theatres of Art*,
   London: Bloomsbury.
Coe, Sebastian. (2013), *Running My Life: The Autobiography*,
   London: Hodder & Stoughton.
Coletti, Theresa. (2004), *Mary Magdalene and the Drama of
   Saints: Theater, Gender, and Religion in Late Medieval England*,
   Philadelphia: University of Pennsylvania Press.
Condon, Janette. (2000), "The Patriotic Children's Treat: Irish
   Nationalism and Children's Culture at the Twilight of Empire,"
   Irish Studies Review, 8 (2): 167–78.
Corney, Frederick C. (2004), *Telling October: Memory and the
   Making of the Bolshevik Revolution*, Ithaca, NY: Cornell
   University Press.
Craig, Hardin. (1955), *English Religious Drama of the Middle Age*s,
   Oxford: Clarendon Press.
Crum, Mason. (1923), *A Guide to Religious Pageantry*, New York:
   Macmillan.
D'Agati, Philip A. (2011), *Nationalism on the World Stage: Cultural
   Performance at the Olympic Games*, Lanham, MD: University
   Press of America.
David, Alfred. (1998), "Noah's Wife's Flood," in James J. Paxson,
   Lawrence M. Clopper, Sylvia Tomasch, and Martin Stevens (eds.),
   *The Performance of Middle English Culture: Essays on Chaucer
   and the Drama in Honor of Martin Stevens*, 97–109, Cambridge:
   Brewer.
Davidson, Clifford. (1996), "Technology in the Medieval Drama,"
   in Davidson (ed.), *Technology, Guilds, and Early English Drama*,
   34–47, Kalamazoo, MI: Medieval Institute Publications.
Davidson, Clifford and Ann E. Nichols. (1989), *Iconoclasm Versus
   Art and Drama*, Kalamazoo, MI: Medieval Institute Publications.
Davis, Caroline Hill. (1916), *Pageants in Great Britain and the
   United States*, New York: New York Public Library.
Davol, Ralph. (1914a), *A Handbook of American Pageantry*,
   Taunton, MA: Davol Publishing.
Davol, Ralph. (1914b), "Pageantry as a Fine Art," *Art and Progress*,
   5 (8): 299–303.

Dean, Joan FitzPatrick. (2014), *All Dressed Up: Modern Irish Historical Pageantry*, Syracuse, NY: Syracuse University Press.

Denney, Colleen. (2018), *The Visual Culture of Women's Activism in London, Paris and Beyond: An Analytical Art History, 1860 to the Present*, Jefferson, NC: McFarland.

Dillon, Janette. (1998), *Language and Stage in Medieval and Renaissance England*, Cambridge: Cambridge University Press.

Dolan, Terence Patrick (2005), "The Mass as Performance Text," in John A. Alford (ed.), *From Page to Performance: Essays in Early English Drama*, 13–24, East Lansing: Michigan State University Press.

Dorr, Rheta Childe. (1909), "What Eight Million Women Want," *Hampton Magazine*, 23 (August): 3.

Downing, Taylor. (2012), *Olympia*, London: BFI Publications.

DuBois, Ellen Carol. (2020), *Suffrage*, New York: Simon & Schuster.

Duffy, Eamon. (2006), *The Stripping of the Altars: Traditional Religion in England, c.1400–c.1580*, New Haven, CT: Yale University Press.

Dunham, Brent (ed.). (2011), *Danny Boyle: Interviews*, Jackson: University of Mississippi Press.

DuToit, H. C. (2009), *Pageants and Processions: Images and Idiom as Spectacle*, Newcastle upon Tyne: Cambridge Scholars.

Eisler, Garrett. (2016), "'Ethnic Americanism' versus Isolationism: Pluralistic Antifascism in 'Fun to Be Free' (1941)," in Cheryl Black and Jonathan Shandell (eds.), *Experiments in Democracy: Interracial and Cross–Cultural Exchange in American Theatre, 1912–1945*, 191–212, Carbondale: Southern Illinois University Press.

Esty, Jed. (2009), *A Shrinking Island: Modernism and National Culture in England*, Princeton, NJ: Princeton University Press.

Evreinov, Nikolaï Nikolaevich, Inke Arns, Igor M. Chubarov, Sylvia Sasse, Bernard Heise, David Riff, Jordan Lee Schnee, and Andri Hürlemann. (2017), *Nikolai Evreinov and Others: "The Storming of the Winter Palace,"* Chicago: University of Chicago Press.

Farkas, Anna. (2019), *Women's Playwriting and the Women's Movement, 1890–1918*, London: Routledge.

Fawcett, Millicent Garrett. (1908), "To the Editor of the Times," [London] *Times*, June 15: 9.

Fischer-Lichte, Erika. (2005), *Theatre, Sacrifice, Ritual: Exploring Forms of Political Theatre*, London: Routledge.

Fischer-Lichte, Erika. (2008), *History of European Drama and Theatre*, London: Routledge.

Fischer-Lichte, Erika and Jo Riley. (1997), *The Show and the Gaze of Theatre: A European Perspective*, Iowa City: University of Iowa Press.

Fitzgerald, Christina M. (2003), "Manning the Ark in York and Chester," *Exemplaria*, 15 (2): 351–84.

Forsyth, Janice, Kevin Young, and Kevin B. Wamsley. (2005), *Global Olympics: Historical and Sociological Studies of the Modern Games*, Research in the Sociology of Sport, Amsterdam: JAI Press.

Fowler, David C. (2018), *The Bible in Early English Literature*, Seattle: University of Washington Press.

Freeman, Mark. (2013), "'Splendid Display; Pompous Spectacle': Historical Pageants in Twentieth-Century Britain," *Social History*, 38 (4): 423–55.

French, Thomas. (2003), *York Minster: The Great East Window*, Oxford: Oxford University Press.

Gale, Maggie. (1996), *West End Women: Women and the London Stage 1918–1962*, London: Routledge.

Gardiner, Harold C. (1967), *Mysteries' End: An Investigation of the Last Days of the Medieval Religious Stage*, New Haven, CT: Yale University Press.

Gardner, Viv. (1985), *Sketches from the Actresses' Franchise League*, Nottingham: University of Nottingham, Department of English.

Geertz, Clifford. (1973), *The Interpretation of Cultures*, New York: Basic Books.

Glassberg, David. (1990), *American Historical Pageantry: The Uses of Tradition in Early Twentieth Century*, Chapel Hill: University of North Carolina Press.

Golin, Steve. (1988), *The Fragile Bridge: Paterson Silk Strike, 1913*, Philadelphia: Temple University Press.

Green, Martin. (1989), *New York 1913: The Armory Show and the Paterson Strike Pageant*, New York: Collier.

Hamilton, Cicely. (1907), "How the Vote Was Won," *Women's Franchise*, November 14: 227–9.

Hamilton, Cicely. (1910a), *A Pageant of Great Women*, London: Suffrage Shop.

Hamilton, Cicely. (1910b), "Marching Past," *The Vote*, June 25: 105.

Hamilton, Cicely. (1920), *William, An Englishman*, New York:
    Frederick A. Stokes.

Hamilton, Cicely. (1935), *Life Errant*, London: Dent.

Hamilton, Cicely. (1948), *A Pageant of Great Women*, London: M.
    Lawson for the Suffragette Fellowship.

Hamilton, Cicely. (1949), "Triumphant Women," in Eleanor Adlard
    (ed.), *Edy: Recollections of Edith Craig*, 38–44, London: Muller.

Hamilton, Cicely and C. H. Charlton. (1908), *How the Vote Was
    Won*, London: Women Writers' Suffrage League.

Hamilton, Cicely and Christopher St. John. (1909), *How the Vote
    Was Won: A Play in One Act*, Letchworth: Garden City Press.

Hargreaves, John. (2000), *Freedom for Catalonia?: Catalan
    Nationalism, Spanish Identity, and the Barcelona Olympic
    Games*, Cambridge: Cambridge University Press.

Heal, Felicity. (2007), "Giving and Receiving Royal Progress," in
    Jayne E. Archer, Elizabeth Goldring, and Sarah Knight (eds.), *The
    Progresses, Pageants, and Entertainments of Queen Elizabeth I*,
    46–61, Oxford: Oxford University Press.

Heideking, Jürgen. (1994), "The Federal Processions of 1788
    and the Origins of American Civil Religion," *Soundings: An
    Interdisciplinary Journal*, 77 (3/4): 367–87.

Hewett, Rebecca Coleman. (2010), *Progressive Compromises:
    Performing Gender, Race, and Class in Historical Pageants of 1913*,
    Ph.D. diss., University of Texas at Austin. Available online: https://
    repositories.lib.utexas.edu/handle/2152/ETD-UT-2010-05-967.

Hill, Ethel. (1909), "Miss Bessie Hatton," *The Vote*, December 23: 100.

Hill, Janet. (2002), *Stages and Playgoers: From Guild Plays to
    Shakespeare*, Montreal: McGill-Queen's University Press.

Hill, Tracey. (2010), *Pageantry and Power: A Cultural History of
    the Early Modern Lord Mayor's Show, 1585–1639*, Manchester:
    Manchester University Press.

Hitchens, Peter. (2012), "Am I an 'Animal', a 'Cow'—or Just Another
    Victim of BBC Bias?," *Mail on Sunday*, August 4. Available
    online: https://www.dailymail.co.uk/debate/article-2183765/Am-
    I-animal-cow–just-victim-BBC-bias.html.

Hobsbawm, Eric J. (1983), "Introduction: Inventing Traditions," in
    Eric J. Hobsbawm and Terence Ranger (eds.), *The Invention of
    Tradition*, 1–14, Cambridge: Cambridge University Press.

Hogan, Jackie. (2003), "Staging the Nation: Gendered and
    Ethnicized Discourses of National Identity in Olympic Opening
    Ceremonies," *Journal of Sport and Social Issues*, 27 (2): 100–23.

Holledge, Julie. (1981), *Innocent Flowers: Women in the Edwardian Theatre*, London: Virago.

Homan, Richard L. (1981), "Ritual Aspects if the York Cycle," *Theatre Journal*, 33 (3): 302–15.

Hopper, Keith. (1996), "Trainspotting: The Choice of a New Generation," *Film* West, 24: 10–14.

Hulme, Tom. (2017), "'A Nation of Town Criers': Civic Publicity and Historical Pageantry in Inter-war Britain," *Urban History*, 44 (2): 270–92.

Isaacson, Walter. (2018), *Leonardo da Vinci: The Biography*, New York: Simon & Schuster.

Isles of Wonder: London 2012 Olympic Games Opening Ceremony, 27 July 2012—Îles Aux Merveilles: Cérémonie D'ouverture des Jeux Olympiques De Londres 2012, Le 27 Juillet 2012. (2012), Teddington: Haymarket Network.

Jackson, Daniel M. (2009), *Popular Opposition to Irish Home Rule in Edwardian Britain*, Liverpool: Liverpool University Press.

Jefferies, Matthew. (2003), *Imperial Culture in Germany, 1871–1918*, Basingstoke: Palgrave Macmillan.

Jennings, Humphrey, Mary-Lou Jennings, and Charles Madge. (2012), *Pandaemonium: 1660–1886: The Coming of the Machine As Seen by Contemporary Observers*, London: Icon.

Johnston, Alexandra F. (2017), "English Biblical Drama," in Pamela M. King (ed.), *The Routledge Research Companion to Early Drama and Performance*, 187–204, London: Routledge.

Johnston, Alexandra F. and Margaret Dorrell. (1971), "The Doomsday Pageant of the York Mercers, 1433," *Leeds Studies in English*, n.s., 5: 29–34.

Kelly, Katherine. (2004), "Seeing Through Spectacles: The Woman Suffrage Movement and London Newspapers, 1906–13," *European Journal of Women's Studies*, 11 (3): 327–53.

Kelly, Katherine E. (2007), "Gender and Collaboration in Modern Drama," in Bonnie Kime Scott (ed.), *Gender in Modernism: New Geographies, Complex Intersections*, 677–8, Urbana: University of Illinois Press.

King, Frederick D. (2019), "*The Pageant* (1896–1897): An Overview," *Pageant Digital Edition, Yellow Nineties 2.0*, Lorraine Janzen Kooistra (ed.), Ryerson University Centre for Digital Humanities. Available online: https://1890s.ca/pageant_overview/.

King, Pamela M. (2000), "The York Plays and the Feast of Corpus Christi," *Medieval English Theatre*, 22: 13–32.

Kipling, Gordon. (1997), "Anne Boleyn's Royal Entry into London," in Alexandra F. Johnston and Wim Hüsken (eds.), *Civic Ritual and Drama*, 39–78, Amsterdam: Rodopi.

Kiser, Lisa J. (2011), "The Animals in Chester's 'Noah's Flood'," *Early Theatre*, 14 (1): 15–44.

Klaić, Dragan. (2013), *Resetting the Stage: Public Theatre between the Market and Democracy*, Bristol: Intellect.

Kolve, Verdel A. (1980), *The Play Called Corpus Christi*, Stanford, CA: Stanford University Press.

Lacey, Robert. (2002), *Monarch: The Life and Reign of Elizabeth II*, New York: Simon & Schuster.

Lane, Anthony. (2008), "The Only Games in Town," *New Yorker*, August 25, 84 (25): 26–30.

Langdon, William C. (1912), *Celebration of the Fourth of July by Means of Pageantry*, New York: Russell Sage Foundation.

Lau, Meghan. (2011), "Performing History: The War-Time Pageants of Louis Napoleon Parker," *Modern Drama*, 53 (3): 265–86.

Lee, Annisa Lai. (2010), "Did the Olympics Help the Nation Branding of China? Comparing Public Perception of China with the Olympics before and after the 2008 Beijing Olympics in Hong Kong," *Place Branding and Public Democracy*, 6 (3): 207–27.

Leneman, Leah. (1995), *"A Guid Cause": The Women's Suffrage Movement in Scotland*, Edinburgh: Mercat Press.

Lenskyj, Helen. (2002), *The Best Olympics Ever?: Social Impacts of Sydney 2000*, Albany: State University of New York Press.

Lepore, Jill. (2019), *This America: The Case for the Nation*, New York: Liveright Publishing.

Logan, Philip C. (2011), *Humphrey Jennings and British Documentary Film: A Re-assessment*, London: Routledge.

Lumsden, Linda J. (1997), *Rampant Women: Suffragists and the Right of Assembly*, Knoxville: University of Tennessee Press.

MacAloon, John J. (1984), *Rite, Drama, Festival, Spectacle: Rehearsals Toward a Theory of Cultural Performance*, Philadelphia: Institute for the Study of Human Issues.

MacAloon, John J. (2008), *This Great Symbol: Pierre De Coubertin and the Origins of the Modern Olympic Games*, London: Routledge.

McBrinn, Joseph. (2006), "The 1904 Feis na nGleann: Craftwork, Folk Life and National Identity," *Folk Life–Journal of Ethnological Studies*, 45 (1): 24–39.

MacKaye, Hazel. (1914a), *71st Regiment Armory: Men's League for Woman Suffrage of the State of New York, in Collaboration with the Equal Franchise Society, Presents a Pageant Written and Directed by Hazel MacKaye*, [*The American Woman: Six Periods of American Life*], New York: Men's League for Woman Suffrage of the State of New York.

MacKaye, Hazel. (1914b), "Pageants As a Means of Suffrage Propaganda," *The Suffragist* [Washington, DC], 2 (48): 6–7.

MacKaye, Percy. (1912a), *The Civic Theatre in Relation to the Redemption of Leisure: A Book of Suggestions*, New York: Kennerley.

MacKaye, Percy. (1912b), *To-morrow*, New York: Frederick A. Stokes.

MacKaye, Percy. (1915), *The New Citizenship: A Civic Ritual Devised for Places of Public Meeting in America*, New York: Macmillan.

MacKaye, Percy. (1916), *Caliban by the Yellow Sands*, Garden City: Doubleday.

Madsen, Annelise K. (2014), "Columbia and Her Foot Soldiers: Civic Art and the Demand for Change at the 1913 Suffrage Pageant-Procession," *Winterthur Portfolio*, 48 (4): 283–310.

Mathis-Lilley, Ben. (2014), "The IOC Demands That Helped Push Norway Out of Winter Olympic Bidding Are Hilarious," *Slate*, October 2.

Mills, David. (2008), "The Chester Cycle," in Richard Beadle and Alan J. Fletcher (eds.), *The Cambridge Companion to Medieval English Theatre*, 125–51, Cambridge: Cambridge University Press.

Moran, Seán. (2017), *The Stage Career of Cicely Hamilton (1895–1914)*, London: Peter Lang.

Muir, Lynette R. (1995), *The Biblical Drama of Medieval Europe*, Cambridge: Cambridge University Press.

Muir, Lynette R. (2007), *Love and Conflict in Medieval Drama*, Cambridge: Cambridge University Press.

Nelson, Carolyn Christensen. (2008), *Literature of the Women's Suffrage Campaign in England*, Peterborough, ON: Broadview Press.

Nicoll, Allardyce. (1963), *Masks, Mimes and Miracles*, New York: Copper Square.

Nora, Pierre and Lawrence D. Kritzman, eds. (1996), *Realms of Memory: Rethinking the French Past*, New York: Columbia University Press.

Normington, Katie. (2009), *Medieval English Drama: Performance and Spectatorship*, Cambridge: Polity.

Oakshott, Jane. (2013), "The Fortune of Wheels: Pageant Staging Rediscovered," *Yearbook of English Studies*, 43: 367–73.

Orgel, Stephen. (1971), "The Poetics of Spectacle," *New Literary History*, 2 (3): 367–89.

Orgel, Stephen. (1975), *The Illusion of Power: Political Theatre in the English Renaissance*, Berkeley: University of California Press.

Orgel, Stephen. (2011), *Spectacular Performances: Essays on Theatre, Imagery, Books and Selves in Early Modern England*, Manchester: Manchester University Press.

Owens, Gary. (1999), "Nationalism without Words: Symbolism and Ritual Behaviour in the Real 'Monster Meetings' of 1843–45," in Kerby Miller and James Donnelly (eds.), *Irish Popular Culture*, 242–69, Dublin: Irish Academic Press.

Ozouf, Mona. (1994), *Festivals and the French Revolution*, Cambridge, MA: Harvard University Press.

Panofsky, Erwin and Suger. (1946), *Abbot Suger on the Abbey Church of St. Denis and Its Art Treasures*, Princeton, NJ: Princeton University Press.

Parker, Louis Napoleon. (1898), *Souvenir of Three Wagner Cycles at the Royal Opera House, Covent Garden*, 3 vols, London: Harrison and Sons.

Parker, Louis Napoleon. (1905), "Historical Pageants," *Journal of the Royal Society of Arts*, 54: 145.

Parker, Louis Napoleon. (1906), *The Warwick Pageant, July 2, 3, 4, 5, 6, 7, 1906 in Celebration of the Thousandth Anniversary of the Conquest of Mercia by Queen Ethelfleda*, Warwick: Evans and Co.

Parker, Louis Napoleon. (1928), *Several of My Lives*, London: Chapman and Hall.

Paster, Gail Kern. (2011), "The Idea of London in Masque and Pageant," in David Bergeron (ed.), *Pageantry in the Shakespearean Theater*, 48–64, Athens: University of Georgia Press.

Paxson, James J. (1995), "The Structure of Anachronism and the Middle English Mystery Play," *Mediaevalia*, 18: 321–40.

Pethick, Mrs. Lawrence. (1909), "The Purple, White, & Green," in *The Women's Exhibition 1909*, London: Women's Press.

Prevots, Naima. (1990), *American Pageantry: A Movement for Art and Democracy*, Ann Arbor, MI: UMI Research Press.

Purvis, John Stanley (1957), *The York Cycle of Mystery Plays: A Complete Version*, London: S.P.C.K.

Readman, Paul. (2005), "The Place of the Past in English Culture: 1890–1914," *Past & Present*, 186 (February): 147–99.

Rice, Nicole R. and Margaret A. Pappano. (2015), *The Civic Cycles: Artisan Drama and Identity in Premodern England*, South Bend, IN: Notre Dame University Press.

Richards, Steve. (2012), "Don't Laugh, Politicians Deserve Pity Not Ridicule", *The Independent*, August 2. Available online: https://www.independent.co.uk/voices/commentators/steve-richards/steve-richards-dont-laugh-politicians-deserve-pity-not-ridicule-7999205.html.

Roberts, Rebecca B. (2017), *Suffragists in Washington, D.C.: The 1913 Parade and the Fight for the Vote*, Charleston, SC: History Press.

Robins, Elizabeth. (1913), *Way Stations*, New York: Dodd, Mead.

Robinson, John William. (1991), *Studies in Fifteenth-Century Stagecraft*, Kalamazoo, MI: Medieval Institute Publications.

Roche, Maurice. (2000), *Mega-events and Modernity: Olympics and Expos in the Growth of Global Culture*, London: Routledge.

Rockwell, David and Bruce Mau. (2006), *Spectacle*, New York: Phaidon.

Rockwell, Ethel G. (1916), *Historical Pageantry: A Treatise and a Bibliography*, Madison, WI: State Historical Society of Wisconsin.

Rogerson, Margaret. (2011), *The York Mystery Plays: Performance in the City*, Woodbridge: York Medieval Press.

Russell, Phillips. (1913), "The World's Greatest Labor Play: The Paterson Strike Pageant," *International Socialist Review*, 14 (1): 7–9.

Ruwitch, John. (2008), "World Media Hails Beijing's Perfect Night," *Reuters*, August 8. Available online: https://www.reuters.com/article/us-olympics-opening-reaction-idUSSP12531420080808.

Ryan, Deborah Sugg. (2007), "'Pageantitis': Frank Lascelles' 1907 Oxford Historical Pageant, Visual Spectacle and Popular Memory," *Visual Culture in Britain*, 8 (2): 63–82.

Ryan, Deborah Sugg. (2017), "Staging the Imperial City: The Pageant of London, 1911," in Felix Driver and David Gilbert (eds.), *Imperial Cities: Landscape, Display and Identity*, 117–35, Manchester: Manchester University Press.

St. John, Christopher. (1909), "The World We Live in: Suffrage on the Stage," *Votes for Women*, November 12: 103.

St. John, Christopher. (1959), *Ethel Smyth: A Biography*, London: Longmans, Green.

Schama, Simon. (1989), *Citizens: A Chronicle of the French Revolution*, New York: Alfred A. Knopf.

Schechner, Richard. (1994), *Between Theater and Anthropology*, Philadelphia: University of Pennsylvania Press.

Schneider, Rebecca. (2011), *Performing Remains: Art and War in Times of Theatrical Reenactment*, New York: Routledge.

Scott, Bonnie Kime. (2013), "Gender in Modernism," in Maroula Joannou (ed.), *The History of British Women's Writing, 1920–1945*, vol. 8, 23–39, Basingstoke: Palgrave Macmillan.

Simkin, John. (2020), "Cicely Hamilton," Spartacus Educational. Available online: https://spartacus-educational.com/WhamiltonC.htm.

Simpson, Sarah H. J. (1925), "The Federal Procession in the City of New York," *New York Historical Quarterly Bulletin*, 9 (2): 39–56.

Skloot, Robert. (1985), "*We Will Never Die*: The Success and Failure of a Holocaust Pageant," *Theatre Journal*, 37 (2): 167–80.

Smith, Anthony Douglas. (2013), *The Nation Made Real: Art and National Identity in Western Europe, 1600–1850*, Oxford: Oxford University Press.

Smith, Kathryn A. (2003), *Art, Identity and Devotion in Fourteenth-Century England: Three Women and Their Books of Hours*, London: The British Library.

Smuts, R. Malcolm. (2005), "Public Ceremony and Royal Charisma: The English Royal Entry in London, 1485–1642," in Lawrence Stone, A. L. Beier, David Cannadine, and James M. Rosenheim (eds.), *The First Modern Society: Essays in English History in Honour of Lawrence Stone*, 65–94, Cambridge: Cambridge University Press.

Southern, Richard. (1977), *The Seven Ages of the Theatre*, London: Faber & Faber.

Stevens, Martin. (1972), "The York Cycle: From Procession to Play," *Leeds Studies in English*, n.s., 6: 37–61.

Stevens, Martin. (1987), *Four Middle English Mystery Cycles*, Princeton, NJ: Princeton University Press.

Stevens, Thomas Wood. (1917), *The Drawing of the Sword: A Pageant for the Present Hour*, Chicago: Stage Guild.

Strong, Roy. (1986), *Art and Power: Renaissance Festivals, 1450–1650*, Woodbridge: Boydell.

Strong, Roy. (1995), *The Tudor and Stuart Monarchy*, 3 vols, Woodbridge: Boydell & Bower.

Taylor, Diane. (2003), *The Archive and The Repertoire: Performing Cultural Memory in the Americas*, Durham, NC: Duke University Press.

Thomas, Sue. (1995), "Cicely Hamilton on Theatre: A Preliminary Bibliography," *Theatre Notebook*, 49 (2): 99–107.

Tickner, Lisa. (1989), *Imagery of the Suffrage Campaign 1907–14*, London: Chatto.

Tolmie, Jean. (2002), "Mrs Noah and Didactic Abuse," *Early Theatre*, 5 (1): 11–35.

Tolstoy, Vladimir, Irina Bibikova, and Catherine Cooke. (1990), *Street Art of the Revolution: Festivals and Celebrations in Russia 1918–33*, London: Thames and Hudson.

Trimborn, Jürgen. (2008), *Leni Riefenstahl: A Life*, trans. Edna McCown, London: I.B. Tauris.

Turner, Victor. (1988), *The Anthropology of Performance*, New York: Performing Arts Journal Publications.

Twycross, Meg. (2008), "The Theatricality of Medieval English Play," in Richard Beadle and Alan J. Fletcher (eds.), *The Cambridge Companion to Medieval English Theatre*, 26–74, Cambridge: Cambridge University Press.

Twycross, Meg, Sarah Carpenter, and Pamela M. King. (2018), *The Materials of Early Theatre: Sources, Images, and Performance: Shifting Paradigms in Early English Drama Studies*, London: Routledge.

Tydeman, William. (1978), *The Theatre in the Middle Ages: Western European Stage Conditions, c. 800–1576*, Cambridge: Cambridge University Press.

Tydeman, William. (1986), *English Medieval Theatre 1400–1500*, London: Routledge & Kegan Paul.

Tymoczko, Maria. (1995), "Tableaux Vivants in Ireland at the Turn of the Century," *Nineteenth Century Theatre*, 23 (1): 90–110.

Tyson, Cynthia Haldenby. (1974), "Noah's Flood, the River Jordan, the Red Sea: Staging in the Towneley Cycle," *Comparative Drama*, 8 (1): 101–11.

Unger, Richard W. (1992), *The Art of Medieval Technology*, New Brunswick, NJ: Rutgers University Press.

Vandrei, Martha. (2018), *Queen Boudica and Historical Culture in Britain: An Image of Truth*, Oxford: Oxford University Press.

Von Geldern, James. (1993), *Bolshevik Festivals, 1917–1920*,
    Berkeley: University of California Press.
Wagg, Stephen. (2015), "'Isambard Kingdom Brunel Wasn't a
    Marxist': The Opening Ceremony of London 2012," in Stephen
    Wagg (ed.), *The London Olympics of 2012*, 61–89, Global
    Culture and Sport Series, London: Palgrave Macmillan.
Walker, Greg. (2008), "The Cultural Work of Early Drama," in
    Richard Beadle and Alan J. Fletcher (eds.), *The Cambridge
    Companion to Medieval English Theatre*, 75–98, Cambridge:
    Cambridge University Press.
Wallis, Mick. (1994), "Pageantry and the Popular Front: Ideological
    Production in the 'Thirties'," *New Theatre Quarterly*, 10:
    132–56.
Wallis, Mick. (1995), "The Popular Front Pageant: Its Emergence
    and Decline," *New Theatre Quarterly*, 11: 17–32.
Wallis, Mick. (2000), "Delving the Levels of Memory and Dressing
    Up the Past," in Clive Barker and Maggie B. Gale (eds.), *British
    Theatre between the Wars 1918–1939*, 190–214, Cambridge:
    Cambridge University Press.
Ware, Susan. (2019), *Why They Marched: Untold Stories of the
    Women Who Fought for the Right to Vote*, Cambridge, MA:
    Harvard University Press.
Whitelaw, Lis. (1990), *The Life and Rebellious Times of Cicely
    Hamilton*, London: Women's Press.
Whitfield, Stephen J. (1996), "The Politics of Pageantry, 1936–
    1946," *American Jewish History*, 84 (3): 221–51.
Wiebe, Heather. (2006), 'Benjamin Britten, the "National Faith," and
    the Animation of History in 1950s England', *Representations*, 93
    (1): 76–105.
Wildman, Charlotte. (2016), *Urban Redevelopment and Modernity
    in Liverpool and Manchester, 1918–1939*, London: Bloomsbury.
Wiles, David. (2001), "Theatre in Roman and Christian Europe,"
    in John Russell Brown (ed.), *The Oxford Illustrated History of
    Theatre*, 49–92, Oxford: Oxford University Press.
Wiles, David. (2011), *Theatre and Citizenship*, Cambridge:
    Cambridge University Press.
Williams, Richard. (2012), "Boyle's Inventive Ceremony Grabs the
    Licence… and Thrills," *Guardian*, July 28.
Withington, Robert. (1912), *A Manual of Pageantry*, Bloomington,
    IN: Indiana University Extension Service.

Withington, Robert. (1918–1920), *English Pageantry, An Historical Outline*, 2 vols, Cambridge, MA: Harvard University Press.

Withington, Robert. (1939), "Louis Napoleon Parker," *New England Quarterly*, 12 (3): 510–20.

Woodfield, James. (1984), *British Theatre in Transition, 1889–1914*, Totowa, NJ: Barnes & Noble.

Woods, Michael. (1999), "Performing Power: Local Politics and the Taunton Pageant of 1928," *Journal of Historical Geography*, 25 (1): 57–74.

Woolf, Rosemary. (1980), *The English Mystery Plays*, Berkeley: University of California Press.

Wright, Patrick. (1985), *On Living in an Old Country: The National Past in Contemporary Britain*, London: Verso.

Wyatt, Diana. (2013), "Arts, Crafts and Authorities: Textual and Contextual Evidence for North-Eastern English Noah Plays," *Yearbook of English Studies*, 43: 48–68.

Yeats, W. B. (1956), "The Statues," *The Collected Poems of W. B. Yeats*, New York: Macmillan.

Yoshino, Ayako. (2003), "Between the Acts and Louis Napoleon Parker: The Creator of the Modern English Pageant," *Critical Survey*, 15 (2): 49–60.

Zimbalist, Andrew. (2015), *Circus Maximus: The Economic Gamble Behind Hosting the Olympics and the World Cup*, Washington, DC: Brookings Institution Press.

INDEX